To Maric

With all best wishes

Dorothy xx

The Mauricewood Devils

The Mauricewood Devils

Dorothy Alexander

FREIGHT
BOOKS

First published 2016

Freight Books
49–53 Virginia Street
Glasgow, G1 1TS
www.freightbooks.co.uk

Copyright © 2016 Dorothy Alexander

The moral right of Dorothy Alexander to be identified as the author of this work has been asserted by her in accordance with the Copyright, Designs and Patents Act, 1988.

All rights reserved. No part of this publication may be reproduced or transmitted in any form by any means, electronic or mechanical, including photocopying, recording or any information storage or retrieval system, without either prior permission in writing from the publisher or by licence, permitting restricted copying. In the United Kingdom such licences are issued by the Copyright Licensing Agency, 90 Tottenham Court Road, London W1P 0LP.

All the characters in this book are fictitious and any resemblance to actual persons, living or dead, is purely coincidental. A CIP catalogue reference for this book is available from the British Library.

ISBN 978-1-910449-66-0
eISBN 978-1-910449-67-7

Typeset by Freight in Plantin
Printed and bound by Bell and Bain, Glasgow

the publisher acknowledges investment from
Creative Scotland toward the publication of this book

Dorothy Alexander lives and works in the Scottish Borders. A graduate of Glasgow Creative Writing programmes, she writes in Scots and English and is an enthusiastic practitioner of experimental techniques. Her found poetry has been exhibited as visual art and she frequently collaborates with other visual artists. *The Mauricewood Devils* is informed by a long term project based on oral narrative tradition. In 2002 she won the Macallan/*Scotland on Sunday* Short Story Competition.

Dedicated to the memory of the sixty three men and boys killed in the Mauricewood Pit Disaster of 1889.

Also to the memory of Martha Brown Pryde Anderson, my great-grandmother, and of Robert Bowman Robb, my Dad; and to Ellen, David, Euan and Amy who carry them into the future.

Where about the graves of the martyrs. *The whaups are calling.*
My heart remembers how!

[Extract from *The Whaups* by Robert Louis Stevenson,
dedicated to Samuel Rutherford Crockett.]

In an upper room two women sat looking out at the rain.
The younger held the hand of the elder; but in this room also
there was silence. They were silent, for they had seen their
old life crumble like a swallow's nest in the rain, and they
had not yet seen the possibility of any new life rise before
them. So they sat and looked at the rain, and it seemed that
there was nothing for them to do but to go forward forever
and ever the rain beating about them, their feet deep down
in a drift of dead leaves.

[From *The Glen Kells Short Leet* in *The Stickit Minister*, by
Samuel Rutherford Crockett.]

Martha: 1889

Martha spat earth from her mouth as she awoke. Her body was held down so that she couldn't move and a metallic dread jangled through her.

Martha couldn't breathe; air had become solid heat. She was in a tunnel; wooden battens held up the roof. There was a bright light at the far end that flickered red and orange and yellow, and a crackling noise that turned into a roar as a rush of scorching fire slammed into her. The walls of the tunnel were black. They glittered in the light and threw out flames as the burning air swept over them, flames that caught her hair and turned her into a livid candle.

Martha floated inside a tunnel half-filled with water. A soft yellow light shone on the water as it slurped against the tunnel walls. She looked to see if the water moved against anything other than stone, or coal, or wood. Then, up ahead, she could see her Dad. He was crouched on a ledge just above the level of the water. Martha tried to get to where he was but it was as if the more energy she expended, the slower her movements became until her arms and legs became held fast and she had the feeling that the water had turned into a thick jelly. She shouted, Dad, Dad, and he turned to look at her. Martha, I'm over here. He had a bunch of daffodils in his hand. They glowed. He picked off the soft yellow petals one at a time and put them in his mouth. He chewed them up and swallowed them. Dad, Dad, don't eat the pretty flowers. They might be poisonous. They're good, Martha, lovely and juicy. Dad, Dad, don't eat all the pretty flowers; we'll lose the light. Don't worry, there's plenty more where they came from. Martha woke up with his voice in her ears, the sound of it comforting her through a distress that pulsed wildly and was textured like drowning.

It must have been in the week after the Disaster, I had a funny dream one night. I never usually remember my dreams but this one stayed with me; I remember telling my sister Helen about it. It was only years after that I wondered if that was the night our Dad died. I dreamt that my mother appeared. I knew it was her because she had on a blue blouse and her hair was the same shade as mine, just a bit darker. Is that you Mother, I said, and she smiled. Have you come for me? She never spoke, just turned round and started to walk away. All I wanted to do was go after her but I'd heard too many stories about the dead turning up fresh as day at folks' doors and that being the end of them. So I watched her disappear and I woke up with tears streaming down my face because I didn't want her to. It was only later it occurred to me that it might be him she'd come for.

It was September, the first week back at school after the summer holidays. Miss Lillie was my teacher. Young and bright, her name brought me in mind of Lily of the Valley. Mr New, the headmaster, had told the whole school at assembly how well she'd done in her teaching exams. She'd had to go on a Saturday morning up to Peebles to do them. Helen, my sister, was in Miss Mitchell's class because she was two years older than me. Miss Mitchell shouted a lot and had a reputation for being handy with the belt. Poor Helen, she was nervy at the best of times and they'd had to drag her into the classroom on the Monday she was so scared. She never got any better – in fact, she got a hell of a sight worse that year with all that happened. But we knew nothing about what was coming that Thursday as we stopped to throw stones into the Leithen above the Cuddy Brig on our way home.

We ended up late. We'd dawdled down the waterside, stopped to speak to my grandfather's friend Jock Sivis who had a new puppy, such a taking wee thing that louped all over us and nipped our fingers with its sharp teeth, and then we'd had a look in the shop windows along the High Street. Helen always liked looking in Smail the printer's. She liked to see the pictures on the postcards and calendars. She liked the fancy writing on the sample invitations. She'd imagine being invited to a wedding, or a party, or dressing up for a concert. She was always desperate to go to a concert to hear people sing and to have a big box of sweeties to eat while she was listening. I'd never crinkle the paper, Martha, she'd say. I'd be quiet as a mouse. And I liked passing the baker's. My teeth would water at the smells that came out. I was always hungry. Not that we were starved, but I liked my food. I'd have my nose pressed up against the grocer's window, away in a dream, excited at the sight of some new chocolate bar or a big tin of biscuits; they were the kind of things we hardly ever got.

Then we went the long way round by the Traquair Arms. As soon as we got near the house we could see that there was something going on. Our granny was at the gate looking up and down the street and when she saw us she came running, a piece of paper in her hand, screeching where have you been, you pair of inconsiderate and ungrateful wee bitches. She grabbed us both by the arm and shook us, very near lifted us up off the road and shouted at us to get in that house. After all she did for us how could we think to get her so worried and our Dad lost down the mine. She flung us into the kitchen where our grandpa was sitting by the fire with his head in his hands. He looked up and said for God's sake, Jenny, they're only children. That just made her worse. That's no excuse. Their father could be dead and they're dawdling home. And she shook the telegram in front of our faces as she backed us up against the table. Helen stumbled against a chair and fell down. I got my face slapped when I screamed.

That was the first we knew about the Disaster. I know she was upset because she had a soft spot for my dad in as much as she had feelings for anybody. But going on like that... I was only seven years old.

Once she calmed down we got more of the story. A fire had broken out at the pit and trapped more than sixty down the mine – our Dad was one of them. We didn't live with him you see. We'd lived twenty miles away in Innerleithen with his mother and father since I was three weeks old. My granny was always keen to tell me how it was me that killed my mother. How it was me that had brought grief on the family and caused her all the extra work of looking after us when she was at an age when she should be getting some peace and quiet.

That first night we got the news I felt as though someone had pulled my insides out. We'd no tea. We just lay in our bed crying and scared to move. All I could think about was big flames and whether or not my Dad was being roasted alive like the people who go to hell. I couldn't think that he might be dead or, if he wasn't, that he wouldn't get out. I made up stories about how they'd put the fire out and how all the miners were rescued. I was good at making up stories; I had a great imagination. Lying, my granny called it although she had another word for it too, a big word. The first time I heard it I didn't know what it meant. She was plaiting my hair, my head yirked back with every twist, and I was telling her about one of the Sunday School teachers who had called the new woman in the baker's a Jezebel – and I hadn't made that up – when she smacked the side of my head and called me mendacious, said that if I didn't stop that nonsense I'd never get to heaven. But that didn't stop me.

Every night before I went to sleep I'd imagine all sorts of ways to rescue my Dad. That was after we'd said our prayers. My granny would sit on the edge of the bed and say the most of them while me and Helen shut our eyes, clasped our hands together and joined in at the bits we knew. Every night we prayed for God to help us in this difficult hour, for Him to comfort us in our suffering, and for Him to watch over our Dad till he could be restored to us.

Then, once my granny was out the bedroom door, after she'd tucked us in, and she always tucked us in so tight we could hardly breathe, I'd shut my eyes, cuddle Peerie into my chest and restore my Dad. Peerie was the rag doll my Aunty Nellie had made for me when I was born. I kept her in my bed because I'd never been without her when I was wee and she was fragile now.

And by the time I fell asleep my Dad was out and safe and I could feel his arms around me. I could smell the coal and the mustiness of the pit off him and I could see the dirty streaks of black on his skin. In all the stories me and Helen were living in Penicuik with my Dad and Jess; Jess was his second wife. We weren't staying with my granny. We had an upstairs bedroom with a bed each and handmade patchwork quilts on them. We ate the best of food and we sat at the table for our dinner and our tea every day.

Davie Anderson was down the pit and Martha was at the school. Martha didn't have a mummy because she was dead and Martha had never ever seen her. But Davie was the best Daddy that any wee girl could have. He made Martha laugh, he bought sweeties every Saturday and had saved up all his pennies to buy her the loveliest pair of buttoning boots she'd ever seen. She wouldn't swap him for all the tea in China.

On the day of the Disaster the headmaster came in and whispered something to Martha's teacher. She clapped her hand to her mouth and looked as if she was going to faint. There's a fire at the pit, she said. You've all to go home.

Martha and Helen ran straight to the pithead. The firemen put the fire out quick and the miners who hadn't been working that day went down to rescue the men who were trapped. They had to wear scarves round their faces because it was still smoky, and they had big shovels and picks to dig through the coal and the rock. Davie Anderson was stuck underneath a wooden beam that had been holding up the ceiling and had fallen on top of him. They dug him out and carted him back up to the top. Jess was crying when they brought him out because he looked half dead. His face was all scrunched up with pain. It's my leg, my leg. It's awful sore. But the doctor patched it up and told Martha that she had to look after him. So Martha fluffed up his pillow, made him ginger snaps and fetched him cups of tea in his bed until he was better. She let him lean on her when he first started to walk again. She sang My Mother Said to cheer him up.

From that first Thursday my granny was like a too-tight-wound-up thing. Me and Helen tried to keep out of the way as much as we could. We did all our jobs quick and neat and didn't dare ask any questions. My grandfather told us as much as he knew. But the word from Penicuik wasn't good: only dead bodies out and rescuers not able to get down the pit because of the fire. There was to be a big funeral on the Sunday. My granny decided she was going and we were to go with her.

We went to the funerals on the train. That was usually a big treat. As it was, there we were, all toorled up in our Sunday best, me with the buttoning boots that my Dad had bought me and that I was so proud of, not knowing what was ahead of us.

It was misty when we left Innerleithen. My granny had left my grandfather in his bed with a cup of tea, as it was still quite early, and instructions to make sure he got himself to the church to put a word in for Davie. He'd said he would, and I wondered about him as I looked out the train window. It kept me from thinking too much about what we were going to. Would his cough be bad today because his chest was getting worse and he was an awful man to haugh and spit, especially in the mornings? I knew he'd be having a good wash and shave because he liked to be smart to go to church. He'd put on his best white shirt, his Sunday waistcoat with the silver pocket watch, then he'd rub hair tonic into his scalp before he combed his hair and put on his bonnet. I can still see the greasy mark that made.

Me and Helen sooked pandrops and looked out the window while my granny told anyone who would listen about our tragedy. She would nod in our direction, mouth the word *orphans* and shake her head as their faces crumpled up with pity. They all knew about the Disaster. A lot of them were going to Penicuik to see the funerals for themselves. I was just happy not to have to go to church. There were times

I got sick of it. I'd sit there, listening to the minister drone on, spinning out my pandrops. For a good job I liked the singing. And I liked the smells in the church: polish, flowers, dust. But I didn't like the way the stained glass kept the light out. The Catholics go on about Purgatory but you wouldn't have needed to explain it to me sitting in that church on a sunny day. I liked to look at people's clothes and the fancy hats. Mrs Smail had one I loved to look at; it was made of dark green velvet folded soft around the crown and held on with the daintiest jet hat pins. Summer was best. You could see the dresses better then. The new bank manager's wife was always well tricked out. She must've bought her clothes in Edinburgh. She had one dress that I'd have given my eye teeth for. It was sky blue with a satin sheen to it and the fanciest pintuck detailing. I don't think I'd ever hear the Minister if I could see her. In my mind, I'd be prancing up and down the High Street in that dress, a smile for everyone, passing the time of day with anyone who'd stop and give me the chance to be seen. But I didn't like the way the women in the fancy clothes treated us. They never invited my granny to join the Guild and I know that hurt her, she would never have asked, but they were quick enough to take the cakes she baked for their sales of work and her bits of knitting.

Jess was at the station to meet us. I'd never seen her looking like she did. I was so used to seeing her smile and laugh that I couldn't stop looking at her face, looking at the look on her face. It was like she wasn't there and I very much needed her to be there. And she knew that because every now and then she'd give me a cuddle.

It was worse than we'd ever imagined. Penicuik was heaving for a start; it's a wonder me and Helen didn't get lost. Crowds were already gathering as we trailed behind our Granny and Jess to the house where Jess had food ready for us. Never mind that I was upset, I just about ate the plate she gave me as well as what was on it. For once my granny didn't give me a row for being greedy. I'd hardly had a thing since the Thursday. Then out onto the street to see the funerals.

I'll never forget it: the thousands upon thousands who lined the streets, the sounds of weeping and wailing, the beautiful horses, the soldiers. I twiddled the button on the jacket of one of the soldiers we were standing behind. It was so shiny. He winked at me when he realised what I was doing. And then the parade set off. Mind you, parade isn't the right word. I suppose it was more of a procession. It was some spectacle: the poor souls that were dead being taken to the burial grounds, their families behind them, followed by ministers, soldiers, dignitaries, other hangers on, and the Salvation Army. For ages after I wanted to join the Salvation Army, all that singing and banging the tambourine, the uniform with the ribboned bonnets. My granny knocked that out of me; we went to the Parish Church and that was that.

We didn't follow the procession to the cemetery. We watched them all go by then headed back to Jess's. I don't remember an awful lot but what I do remember is being very jealous of the other two girls who were with us: Jess's pal Sadie's two daughters. They'd lost their dad too but at least they still had their mother. I remember feeling claustrophobic in amongst all the people that were on the streets and the relief when we got away from them. That and the big slice of gingerbread that Jess sent us home with. I was going to give it to my grandfather, and I was so excited, so looking forward to seeing his face when I did. But when we got back it was plain to see that he'd never been out of the house. He'd been nowhere near the church. That got my granny started right away. You old devil she called him, lazy, good for nothing waster that couldn't even be bothered to go and put a word in for his own son. But, and this didn't happen often, he stood his ground and said to her, quiet like, but in a tone of voice that let you know he wasn't to be messed with, I'd no heart to go in among a crowd of people all asking about Davie. I'm sure God'll hear what I've got to say whether I'm in a church or not. She never said another word to him, just turned to us and told us to get ready for bed. Then she spied the gingerbread that Jess had given us wrapped up in brown paper, grabbed it out of my hand and flung it in the fire.

Davie Anderson was down the pit and Martha was at the school. Martha was practising cross-stitch when the headmaster came in and whispered something to her teacher. The teacher clapped her hand to her mouth and looked as if she was going to faint. There's a fire at the pit, she said. You've all to go home.

Martha and Helen ran straight to the pithead. All the men who were stuck down the pit had managed to get into a place where there wasn't any fire. They were busy digging a tunnel. They had their piece boxes so they weren't starving. They just had to eat a little bit at a time – one mouthful and chew it as long as they could. Those who had meat pieces shared them out first because they would be the most likely to go off. Cheese would last longer and they'd just have to put up with it going greasy or drying out.

That was the night Helen peed the bed. Something she hadn't done since before she went to the school. I woke up convinced that we were both sitting in the Leithen but amazed because the water was warm. And then, when I realised what it was, I panicked. Helen was still sound asleep and my mind was racing because I knew we'd be for it when my granny found out. I thought I could maybe fold the wet sheet up and get Phamie's mother to wash it for us on the quiet along with our nightdresses. Phamie lived just down the street. She'd two brothers and three sisters and a mother and father that I adored. It was another world in their house; I'd be there as often as I could. Phamie's father worked on the railway, Alex his name was. People called him Big Alex because he was a big man, a gentle giant. He always called me Mattie and would give me a cheery welcome when I came into the house. He smelled of peppermints, peppermints and warm serge. He always had a bag of pandrops in his jacket pocket; he said they helped him concentrate on his timetables. He wasn't one for handing them out. He would never have had any with all the children that ran about his house. But now and then, if I was at their house on a Saturday, he'd slip me a couple on the quiet to take to the church on Sunday. That'll help keep you waken during the sermon he'd say. He was a bit of a heathen, Alex, never needed any persuading to work on a Sunday. At least that was what my granny would say: you've been round at that heathen Alex Sanderson's again. Anyway, I was sure that Phamie's mother would wash the stuff for us and all I had to think about was how to get them out of the house without my granny noticing. But that plan got stuck when I couldn't work out how I'd ever manage to hide a huge bundle like that because our bedroom opened onto the kitchen. Well, we called it the kitchen but it was more like a living room that we cooked, ate, and sat in because the big range fire was there. Our bedroom was really just a box room off it. The people who lived there before us had it as a small workroom because the woman did dressmaking but then her mother came to stay with them and she'd died there. Me and Helen would often scare ourselves stupid imagining her ghost in the room. We'd lie in the dark and at the least noise we'd grip onto one another. We'd be gallous in the daytime, telling our friends about how we'd seen her white frilly bonnet, two staring eyes and hands like claws, how we'd heard the wind whistling through the room that was her soul flying out the window.

By this time, Helen was awake. Just at that my granny came in and she could see something was wrong. She hauled the covers off us and Helen was about through the wall trying to get as far away from her as she could. So I piped up – I spilt the chanty in the middle of the night.

Many's the day after that we both smelled of pee when we went to school. And there were always those who had to be nasty. Peggy Simmons and her crowd held their noses if they saw us. They would shout things like I didn't know the school had a tomcat, and then torment us about our Dad, saying that he was dead and that we were orphans, that we'd soon be in the poor house.

Well I got very angry at them saying my Dad was dead when we didn't know for sure that he was. I hoped against hope for many's a long day, right up until they found him and that was a good six months. Miss Lillie was kind. She would often ask us how things were and one time she brought us some clothes. She didn't give us them in front of everyone. She came to the house. My granny was none too pleased; she was a proud woman. We were sent through to our bedroom and the door shut but we could still hear the most of what was said. Miss Lillie charmed my granny good-style. Told her what a credit we were to her and that no one would ever need to know where the clothes came from. I don't know where she got them. Whether she'd maybe even bought them herself with her own money. She said they were her niece's. That her sister had married well to a man who worked in the bank in

Galashiels and was pleased to see the clothes going to good use. When I thought about it later though, it was maybe just too good to be true that the one niece's clothes fitted the both of us, but there you go. I never forgot her for doing that. I remember the clothes smelled as if they'd been ironed with lavender water.

There was a knock at the door one Saturday afternoon and there was Jess. My granny had known she was coming but hadn't told us. Helen and I were so pleased to see her although we were always shy at first because we didn't dare make a show of ourselves. She'd brought us some sweets and a piece of ribbon each for our hair, the same kinds of things that she'd have brought if my Dad was there. And that was the first thing we asked, had they found our Dad. But that was a good few weeks after the first funerals and we could see by her face that that they hadn't. She cuddled us in and the tears streamed down her cheeks so fast that they dripped onto our hair. My granny brought out an old hanky, one of my grandfather's. It was clean, but worn at the edges, a raggy hanky we called it. Here, she said, handing it to Jess, crying like that won't bring him back. Turns out Jess had come down to bring some of the money that people from all over had sent and had been put together in a big fund to help the families. She told us all about what they thought was going to be done with it, that so much money was to be given out every week depending on how many children you had. She wasn't sure how that would happen but even if she had to save it up and bring it down herself, she would. As it turned out, it came through the Post Office. My granny went every week to collect it then she'd come home and rant on about how that was all that was keeping us from the poor house. We were always being threatened with the poor house, with the shame of it. There was a casual house up the Leithen Road and we'd see the kind of people that went in about there, not much more than tramps some of them, and skinny, whey-faced children with mothers that looked like they'd no fight left. It was an empty threat though, she was good with money, my granny. She would have made an excellent book-keeper or a bookie if she'd had a mind!

After Jess had had a cup of tea and told us all the news about the fund, she took us out a walk because it was such a nice day, one of those warm October afternoons when the leaves are turning and everything feels quiet and still. We didn't go far because Jess had to get the train back. She said where do you want to go and I said up the Windyknowe because that was the first hill I ever climbed with my Dad. And of course I had my buttoning boots on that her and my Dad had bought me in the summer.

That day I got them was one of the best days I could ever remember. My Dad and Jess had come down on the train as usual and me and Helen had gone to meet them. Jess had a bonny blouse on, white with sprigs of lilac, and my Dad was in his shirt sleeves, his jacket slung over his shoulder because it was so warm. I was about through myself with excitement because they'd promised me the last time I saw them that they'd bring me a new pair of boots. I'd never had brand-new boots. I'd usually get Helen's cast-offs but her last pair were still too big for me and they were nearly worn out. Not that that was a bother because my grandfather was good at mending shoes. It brought some money in since his rheumatics had got worse – too many years of heavy working outside in all weathers. That's why he'd loved it so much when they'd come to Innerleithen at first. He'd got himself a job in the Leithen Hotel in the High Street, to my granny's disgust. But it was a pleasing change for him. He liked being inside and having people to speak to but there was a lot of heavy lifting and late nights. All I'd ever known him to do was mend shoes or do bits of upholstery. And, because he had a good way with animals through having worked on farms all his young days, people would bring him things they'd found that had got hurt. There were times we had a right menagerie. He kept pigeons, a lot of people did then, and for a long time there was a tame crow in beside them. He'd mended its wing when it was young and it seemed to think it was a pigeon as it never flew away even though it had the chance. Jaikie my grandfather called it because it was a jackdaw. He taught it tricks. Come on, Jaikie, he'd say, let's see you playing golf, and it would pick up a stick and poke scrunched-up paper balls that my grandfather would catch in a tin can as they rolled off the edge of the bench. All the children round about loved seeing Jaikie do that. And it would take small pieces of cheese or bread out of my grandfather's mouth. He would always get a row for that if my granny caught him. It was a dirty trick; he didn't know where that bird's beak had been and it was a waste of cheese into the bargain. It lived a good long time, till my grandfather went out one winter's morning and it was lying dead. We were all heartbroken except my granny. It used to peck her any time it got the chance. It would sit on the window ledge when my grandfather was working in his shed and squawk if it saw her coming out of the house. She'd shout at it, call it the ill-tempered, flea-ridden work of the Devil and threaten it with next door's cat.

But that day I got the boots was a good day. My granny was always pleased to see my Dad and she knew Jess was a good woman even if she was Free Church. So, like I say, Helen and me went to the station to meet them. The only thing I was interested in was the boots. I could see they had them because what else could have been in a parcel that size. All I wanted to do was open it right there and then. Next thing I knew, my Dad had ushered us all into the waiting room so that I could. My excitement fairly amused the people inside. I ripped the paper off and squealed with delight when I pulled them out of their wrapping. I was so happy I burst into tears just as Big Alex was going past the window and he came in to see what all the to do was about. Hell, he said, because he was a terrible man to swear, I thought someone had died there was such a commotion. And I ran up to him, so pleased to show him my new boots. Come on then, he said, let's see you with them on. So, quick as I could, and that wasn't as quick as it might have been what between my fingers being all thumbs and Helen trying to help me and just tangling things up, I got the new boots on and paraded up and down the waiting room. People were so pleased for me that they clapped and said what a lovely pair of boots they were and was I not the luckiest wee lassie in Innerleithen. And that was them on for the day, no matter that we were going up Lee Pen. I'd have slept with them on if they'd let me.

We went a picnic, just the four of us, me and Helen, my Dad and Jess. They'd brought sandwiches with them and a piece of cake, and my Dad stopped in at the Leithen Hotel to get a bottle of beer for himself and lemonade for us. He could hardly get back out for speaking to people. Many's the row Jess gave him when the tea ended up burnt or they were late because he'd been blethering; but that was just him. When he came out you could hear them all laughing at whatever he'd been telling them. I was never as proud as I was that day. My granny just shook her head when we looked in at the house. You're ruining that child – no good'll come of it. But my Dad ignored her and winked at me, said I deserved something nice now and then.

I was used to climbing hills, usually it would be the smaller ones, Caerlee or the Windyknowe, if it was just me and Helen and our friends. But that day we went up Lee Pen. It's one of the biggest round about. You can see it from miles away. You can even see it from Peebles. It's a bonny shape. You get onto it as though you're going up Caerlee then turn right when you cross a drystane dyke. There are sheep on it; they keep the grass down and you can follow their trails. About two thirds of the way up, we came across a big white ball growing out of the ground. Well, I thought it was big. And here it was a mushroom; I'd never seen the like. My Dad knew what it was, a puff-ball he called it, a devil's snuff-box, because the insides turn powdery and puff out into the wind when it's spent. He pulled it out of the ground and held it out to us. Have a sniff at that. It smelled like the most delicate mushroom you could ever imagine. He fried it in butter when we got back because he knew that my granny wouldn't have anything to do with it. We ate it on its own as a treat before we had our tea. It was a beautiful thing, big marshmallowy slices that just melted in your mouth and the loveliest buttery, mushroomy taste. I often look for them yet if I'm out walking at that time of year.

Earlier he'd given it to Helen to carry and once we'd had our picnic it was wrapped in the paper that the sandwiches had been in and laid carefully in Jess's bag. But before that we climbed right to the top. I couldn't believe how blustery it was. I held onto my Dad and Jess because the wind had turned my pinafore into a kite and I was scared I was going to blow away. They laughed at me hanging on for grim death. Then we all oohed and aahed at the scenery, at the views across the town – we picked out the streets and my granny's house – till my Dad said right let's go and make a mess of ourselves with that picnic and we clambered back down to get out of the wind. My Dad had a cold bacon sandwich. I didn't fancy that at all. The thought of eating anything cold and greasy never appealed. I can't remember what the rest of us had, it would be cheese or potted meat most likely, and then a slice of Jess's mother's cherry cake. I remember that clear as day. I'd kept a big, whole cherry for one last mouthful and felt like I'd gone to heaven when I bit into it, it was so sweet and juicy. Then a man appeared up the hill with his dog. I could tell it wasn't someone my Dad knew because, when he spoke to him, he put on his Sunday voice. The man stopped and blethered for a minute or two while his dog stood and panted with the exertion of running up the hill. It was a collie so that got us pestering our Dad to tell us about the dog down the mine shaft. It was a story that our Dad had told us years before when it first happened but we loved nothing better than to hear it again. And by now, Dad had all the actions off pat and he wouldn't dare leave out a single bit.

It was about a boy who came from near Gorebridge who had worked beside my Dad down the pit. He'd been out a walk when he'd heard an animal yelping but for the life of him he couldn't see it. He'd looked and looked under all the bushes, in behind the wall and the trees round about till he realised the noise was coming from what had been an airshaft for one of the mines that was long finished working. It was a dog, a long way down and it was in a terrible state. So he ran back to his mother's house and brought her clothes basket and the longest piece of rope he could find. He stole a piece of meat out of the soup pot to entice the animal with, then ran all the way back to the hole. He tied a big knot and ran the basket down as fast as he could. My Dad would jump up and mime tying a big knot, wiping the sweat off his forehead as he paid the rope out hand over hand until it stopped with a jolt when it hit the bottom. He'd get down on his knees as if it was him at the side of the hole and shout, come on, wee dog, jump in. He'd pull the rope back up when he could feel the weight of the dog in the basket and then nearly fall over when it fell out. This would go on numerous times as me and Helen, and Jess too, roared with laughter at him trying to get the poor dog out of the hole. The boy never gave up, even when people told him to pour stones down and be done with it, he persevered. And he got there. He got the dog out. Eventually, it managed to stay in the basket long enough for him to pull it up and grab hold of it. There was a big stone tied round its neck. No wonder it was so heavy. Someone had flung it down that hole to kill it. Well, the boy took it home. It was a collie cross, a very biddable dog; it went with him when he left the pit to be a gamekeeper. Helen said they were bad those people who wanted to pour stones down the hole, weren't they Dad? And he said yes, but they would be worried that Jimmy couldn't get him out and that he'd suffer. But how would he suffer, Dad? He'd starve. But would he not suffer worse if they poured the stones down on top of him and they just bashed him about? Would that not be worse? And my Dad grabbed her and cuddled her tight and said but we don't need to worry about that, Helen, the dog got out and lived a great life, he's still running about yet. My Dad soon had her laughing again. He ran down the hill, kidded on he was a lamb that had lost its mother and made pitiful baaaing noises. He pretended that Helen was the mother and skipped round about her, getting down on his knees, nuzzling his head into her, his bonnet falling off into the bracken as I skelped his behind and told him he was bad for running away, then he caught me and we rolled about on the grass.

Davie Anderson was down the pit and Martha was at the school. At dinner time on the day of the Disaster, Martha had fallen out with her sister, Helen, over whose turn it was to caw the skipping rope. But when the headmaster brought word that the pit was on fire, Helen grabbed Martha's hand and they ran straight to the pithead. The boys and girls from the school found as many hoses and pipes as they could and joined them all up with special sticky bandages that never leaked and stuck one end in the nearest burn and the other end down the pit and poured water in till the fire went out and the cages came up full of men and boys, all dripping but all smiling and so pleased to have been saved. Martha's and Helen's clothes got all wet when Davie gave them a big cuddle and said that's a right drookin you've given me.

We were remembering these things as we walked along the High Street towards the Windyknowe. Then, once we were on the path up the hill, Jess asked us how we were getting on and did I still play round at Phamie's? So I said yes but I'd stopped dancing. I loved to dance although I only ever did it at Phamie's house. I wouldn't have dared at my granny's; dancing was the work of the Devil. Jess asked how come I'd stopped, and I remember saying, for all I would only be seven years old, that my heart wasn't in it any more. She smiled at that and gripped my hand tighter as we climbed up. It didn't take us long to get to the top and we sat down for a minute or two on hummocks of dry grass to get our puff back.

It's a terrible thing that's happened to us, Jess said. No wonder you don't feel like dancing. She cuddled us both in and the three of us sat there and looked down at the town, at the Tweed as it comes round corner from Peebles and past Traquair before it heads down to Walkerburn, and across to the hills on the other side of the valley that head away to Yarrow and the Lochs. Then she told us a story about her cousin who had been lost at sea. I think she was trying to let us know that she knew how we were feeling and that it was natural to feel like that. He had an unusual name, Urquhart he was called, Urquhart Stevenson, and he'd been a year or so older than Jess, one of her mother's sister's boys. And Jess, not having any brothers, was very fond of her cousins and especially this one. He was a clever boy: could take a clock to bits and put it all back together quick as wink; went to sea hoping to be a navigator but his ship went down on the way home from Adelaide. It was a clipper, a right fast one too, called The Lammermuir. I think his family all thought that was a good omen when they heard the name of it because their house looked out onto the Lammermuirs. But so much for that, only seventeen he was and a good-looking boy, tall and dark and ever so obliging. Jess said that when the word came that he was lost at sea, the hurt went deep inside and she was left feeling numb. A horrible feeling came over her that was like panic and she only realised what it was when she heard the word anguish. And that sounded right, for that was how I felt. She said that for months, years even, she expected him to come up the path to her mother's door with a fantastic tale about how he'd been rescued. Even yet there was a bit of her hoped that might happen someday, that he'd maybe swum to a South Sea island and lived with the folk there, maybe married one of them and never had the inclination or chance to get back. She laughed at the thought. One of her favourite memories of him was on a day when both the families had gone a picnic up the burn at the back of her auntie's house. They'd had a fire going and blankets spread out on the grass to sit on. There had been a big to-do when two of the cousins who'd been carrying a big pot with the dinner in it had tripped and nearly dropped the lot in a cow pat. The children had played all day in the burn. They'd spent most of their time building a dam; the younger ones were sent to fetch stones and clay while the older ones were in charge of the building. Jess shuddered. She said she could still feel the clagginess of the clay as it squidged out of her fingers and turned the water cloudy but they'd had great fun swimming in the pool that the dam made. In Jess's mind, Urquhart had built himself a grand mud hut on his desert island. But he never came home.

Davie Anderson was down the pit and Martha was at the school. When word came that there was a fire, Martha and Helen ran straight to the pithead. The people trying to rescue the miners poured so much water down trying to put the fire out that it was like a river inside the tunnels. Davie Anderson couldn't swim so he'd jumped in a coal cart and floated on top of the water. He'd floated and floated and swirled along till he came to where the cage was and he managed to grab hold of the door and climb in. He signalled for them to pull him up and up he came. There was a big cheer from all the people standing at the top waiting when they saw Davie Anderson's face smiling at them from the bars of the cage. He pulled the door open so fast that he nearly broke it and in less than a minute he had one arm round Helen and the other round Martha and was squeezing them so tight they could hardly breathe.

Jess: 1889 – 1890

The Midlothian coal field forms a basin fifteen miles long that stretches from Carlops out into the Firth of Forth. It is made up of seams of varying thicknesses, all named, lying beneath Blackband ironstone. At Mauricewood they mined the edge coals of the widest of them: the Great Seam.

Mauricewood lay within the estate of the Clerks of Penicuik (the family home of James Clerk Maxwell). On September 5, 1889, fire caused the deaths of sixty-three men and boys, thirty-six of whose bodies were not recovered until March 1890. It was owned and run by the Shotts Iron Company.

In 1889 the Shotts Iron Company was under considerable financial strain: start-up costs at Mauricewood were high; costly litigation instigated by local landowners stopped smelting at the pithead so that all materials now had to be transported to Shotts in Lanarkshire. There had been no shareholder dividend for three years.

A Government Inquiry into the circumstances of the Disaster concluded that it was accidental and attached no blame to the Company. A Supplementary Report issued in April 1890 stated that it was obvious from the position the men were found in that a good number had survived for some time.

1 2 11 [Numbers refer to sources within Author's Notes]

I don't think you ever get over something like Mauricewood. I suppose I was lucky in that the whole town suffered and I had my mother and father and my sister to help me. I wouldn't have coped half as well if I hadn't had them – and Sadie.

Sadie was my best friend from when we were children. We'd stayed in the same street and our mothers were friends. Her father was killed when he was just a young man. He fell off a roof and they brought him home on an old door. After that, my mother would often make an extra lot of soup and I'd be sent over with it in a bowl with a tea towel over the top. I didn't dare trip. Or if she was baking – my mother was a lovely baker – something always went across the road. Sadie was as often as not at our house. She was a right character, full of fun and cheery. She had the bonniest black hair and big brown eyes. She was always small, and I was always bigger than her. And she loved singing. Her father had been a singer; he'd known all the old songs, the bothy ballads, and she was a quick learner, too quick her father said. She shouldn't have been singing some of those songs. We didn't know the half of what they were about. We just giggled because we knew they were about courting and how you got babies and that we didn't dare sing them at Sunday School.

We both started at Harper's paper mill on the same day. My father had word from the foreman to send us down. Sadie got a start collecting shavings; with her being so small they must have thought that she'd be better at getting under and between the machines to pick them up. They started me on the rag picking. I couldn't say which of us worse off. The rags were full of dust from the disinfection powder and I'd breathe it in and half choke sometimes. And the stuff wasn't really clean. It wouldn't be the first time I've come across a dead mouse or dried-in dirt sticking things together. My job was to cut off buttons and hooks and eyes, to cut the bones out of corsets, and get rid of anything sharp or hard that wasn't going into the paper. We lasted about six months there. Sadie left first. She was sick of the fleas! That and doing nothing but crawl about the floor and trail huge bags of shavings from the bottom of the mill to the top. She wasn't scared to speak her mind, Sadie. She told them straight that their mill was dirty and that she was disgusted at having to wash herself out of the same barrel as everybody else before she went home. I left not long after. Sadie had got into Valleyfield and was in the cutting – a cleaner job – cutting the paper as it came off the guillotine and putting it into boxes for the overhaulers. She got me in beside her and we had a great time. It was hard work and we did the same things day in day out but we had a good laugh and it wasn't too long before we got ourselves into the overhauling. We were good workers and we were both smart. The overhauling salle was so clean and big and airy with lots of windows so that we had plenty of light to work in. It was amazing how fast we could check a ream of paper. Although we suffered bad with paper cuts. There would be times when our hands were red raw. My mother bought boracic ointment for me to rub into them. But I was lucky; I was never bothered with dermatitis like some of them were.

We were always together. Saturday afternoons, after we'd got our pay and divvied up at home, we'd go down the street with the money we had left and rake around, maybe buy something for ourselves if we'd saved up enough, maybe some lace to diddle up an old dress if there was a dance that night. Then on Sunday we'd be at Church: Sadie at the Parish, me at the Free, though we never let that bother us. Sadie would call me a Disrupter and I'd tell her that she'd burn in hell with all the rest of them that were damned, but we'd be laughing when we said it.

On Sundays we went to church; we'd put on our best clothes and sit on a hard pew for the best part of two hours. I'd suck pandrops and let my mind wander during the sermon. I'd always try my best to follow the gist of what the Minister was saying but my mind would drift and, as often as not, I'd be dreaming about what I might get up to with Martin Stark if only I could get him to notice me. The Minister would be doing his best to help us stay on the paths of righteousness and I'd be wondering how I might sort my hair for later on when Martin might be in the crowd that went for a stroll to the Roslyn road end.

That was the thing to do on a Sunday night if the weather was fair. All the young ones would walk out there. They'd come from Penicuik, Auchendinny, Roslyn – even some from Loanhead. There would be a good crowd all blethering and carrying on. Many's a couple got together that way. That's where Sadie met Johnny Glass. He'd just come into the town to work in the mine. I still find it hard to say its name. Johnny was lodging with Davie and his first wife, Maggie. He was a fine lad, Johnny Glass; you never heard a cross word out of him. He was the last one they found, a good few days after Davie. I'd never seen Sadie in such a state as that day they got him out. I went with her when she went to identify the body. It wasn't as if she didn't know what to expect. We'd all been looking for our own since they'd started bringing the bodies out. Jimmy Irvine had lain for three days in that shed they used as a mortuary before they decided it must be him. So we'd seen what the six months since the Disaster had done: turned them red with the rust that had seeped out of the ironstone; mummified some so that they looked as if they were still living. But those who had found them warned us not to touch because their skin and hair would just come away in our hands. Some were sprouting fungus... and the smell! They spread chloride of lime all over the floor to mask it. It was hard not to be sick. Sadie was worried that Johnny had been bashed about, and when she went in they had his face covered with sacking.

She made them pull the cover back and nearly fainted at what she saw. Johnny had been handsome. They were a very loving couple. The only way she knew it was him was the top button missing off his shirt. She'd meant to mend it all week before the Disaster. It wasn't as if she didn't have any buttons to mend it with. Everybody in Penicuik had a box of buttons from the mill. Her legs gave way then. The men who were in there held her up and helped me get her back outside. I sat her down on a pile of wood and kept hold of her until she recovered. My mind was racing because I knew that we'd have to get him buried. Bob Grier came across to us to ask if they could coffin him right there and then and what did she want them to do with him because some of the bodies had been taken straight to the cemetery. I'll never forget the look she gave him. I'm not ready for that, she said, I'll need to take him home. Then she turned to me, I need to take him home, Jess. I can't just leave him. Bob took me aside to say that at least two were being buried tomorrow at the Auld Kirkyard. I knew this because I'd spoken to Jimmy Irvine's wife earlier that morning. Jimmy and George Pennycook were being buried and it would be no hardship to bury another one. So, while they put Johnny into a coffin, I took Sadie home. The second time in a week that I'd done that walk only this time it was me doing the supporting. I couldn't remember much about the first time. But now I found myself aware of the first hints of green coming through the grass at the side of the road, of catkins hanging over the fence with what looked like yellow powder dancing on the edges of them. I told her what Bob Grier had said about the two burials in the morning. I tried to get her to see that it would be as good a day as any – that it wouldn't be a good idea to keep him any longer, especially for the children's sake.

Colliers' tools included a hammer or 'mash', a shovel and a pick, a ratchet and drill (which had either a fishtail cutting end for coal or removable studs for stone), and a saw to cut wooden pit props. All these had to be purchased as had any explosives they needed.

The explosive took the form of gunpowder manufactured locally by Messrs Hay, Merricks & Co, at Roslin Powder Mills. The *black pooder* was purchased in either one pound or half pound weight *pirns* which had a small hole through them in which a length of *strum* or fuse was attached.

Gunpowder was highly susceptible to dampness, thus, when ignited below ground, it might emit such vast volumes of smoke that personnel were hastily withdrawn until it cleared. It was not until 1886, when the Nobel Company experimented with gelignite at a colliery in Hamilton, that gunpowder was gradually phased out.

1

The pickaxe was the basic tool of the trade. Different types were used as a combination of hammer, wedge, and crowbar to prise, split, shear and undercut stone and mineral. Made of steel-tipped iron, the heads weighed between two and seven pounds and were attached to variously shaped ash shafts.

The miner had also to provide fuel for his cap lamp. Historically, this took the form of 'sweet oil', then tallow which the mice seemed to thrive on, and eventually paraffin wax, which was purchased in cakes, measuring 6" x 4" x 1" and manufactured by Dixons at Edgefield, Loanhead.

Until 1799, the Midlothian miner had been in legal bondage to the mine owner. Although now free, the Company stopped money from his wages for the services of a blacksmith to sharpen and maintain his tools. It also stopped money for rent and coal for his fire. Rents were high.

The Company operated a contractor system. A miner would enter into a contract with the pit manager to undertake a specific task – drive roadways or extract coal or ironstone for an agreed amount. He would hire workmen at (often exploitative) piecework rates which had a divisive influence on the workforce.

1 2

Sadie's mother was at the house with the girls when we got there. She knew as soon as she saw us what had happened. She was at the door with the youngest in her arms but the other two came running. Have they found our Pa? Have they found him? And Sadie just let out such a wail and gathered them to her. She buried her face in their hair and said yes, they'd found him, he had been the last one. Helen, the oldest, tore herself away from her mother and backed towards the house, her hand muffling the words no, no, no. Agnes put her hand up to Sadie's face and said don't cry, Ma, don't cry. So we got them into the house and I asked one of the neighbours who was outside waiting to hear about Johnny to tell them down at the Mission that they were bringing him home and that we hoped to have him buried tomorrow.

When I went in, her mother was trying to get her to take a glass of brandy. Sadie was beside the fire. The two girls clung onto her. Their hands held tight to her sleeves, to her shawl, to her skirt. They looked scared. Sadie stared into the fire and stroked their hair. Every now and then she shook her head. Come on, her mother was saying, drink this; it'll steady your nerves because they'll be here soon. Sadie took the glass and lifted it to her mouth. She held it there for a second till one of the children moving swilled it against her lips and she downed the lot. Then she got us all organised. Better get the table cleared and out into the middle of the floor. And we'll need to lift that rug and put the good one down, or maybe wait till after to put it down, save too many dirty feet on it. Her mother asked if she wanted her to take the children away. But she said they'd be all right there with her. And was there enough whisky in the cupboard to give those who were bringing him home a dram? And who would tell the Minister that she needed a funeral tomorrow. I told her that I'd sent word to the Mission. They'd help to get things organised because they'd been good right from the start back in September when the first ones were brought out.

Sadie looked towards the door. Is that them now; I thought I heard the sound of horses? She was right enough. When I went to the door there was a cart coming up the street but it was just the man who emptied the middens going home. It's just the scaffie on his way home, I shouted in. It's a wonder you couldn't smell him. Then I felt terrible because I thought about what was coming and the smell it would bring. I looked for the carbolic that I knew she kept in the cupboard above the sink – up high so that the little ones couldn't reach it. I had to think where to put it so that there was no repeat of what happened at the house where Hugh McPherson and his son were laid out. One of their nieces drank it and caused the most terrible commotion.

Hugh and Peter had been the first two to be buried back in September. Hugh was one of the first ones that they found: him and Jock Walker. It was not long after I'd left the pithead and gone home because it looked like no-one was getting out. We'd been waiting there since we first heard there was something wrong.

They'd let us away from the mill when the word came round. I ran like hell along that road, my heart thumping and my stomach in my feet, me and all the other ones with family down the mine. I shouted in at Sadie's but she was away already. I thought she would be. Old women stood outside their doors crying and chewing at the ends of their fingers. I looked up the Edinburgh Road and all I could see was people running, some trailing children behind them. The word wasn't good, there was a fire, two had got out but any others they'd hauled up were dead.

Up the road there was the most awful wailing. People had stopped to stare at a horse and cart as it went by. As I got near, we heard voices shout who is it and I could see people clasp their hands to their mouths with the shock of what they saw. There were four bodies in the back of the cart. Three boys and old Willie Hunter. They had them covered with the canvas that they used down the pit. It was filthy and there wasn't much of it. People were shouting and crying – shouting out names. It's the laddie Foster, his head's all bashed in. No it's not. That looks like one of Geordie Pennycook's. If that's Bob Tolmie's laddie, he's just a bairn. I asked the man who led the horse how many more were dead. But he just shook his head. No more as yet but the smoke was terrible and they were having an awful job trying to get past it. They'd pulled this lot out but the smoke had done for them. I couldn't help but think about what was coming to their families, to their mothers, about what was waiting for me at the pit.

There was a good crowd by this time all hurrying up the hill to Mauricewood. What between the worry and the effort of rushing to get there, even if they were in tears, most of them were quiet. We all knew, but hardly dared say, that there was no other way to get out if the fire was in the main incline. There was supposed to be; it was the new regulations, and the old manager had started a new shaft not long before he finished, but that bugger, Mr John Love, had put a stop to it; it was costing too much. Did we want jobs or not was how he put it. And anyway there was the pipe upset if anybody needed to get out in a hurry as well as the road to Greenlaw pit. That all sounded fine but everyone knew that to climb the pipe upset wasn't easy. It was just a narrow hole with a ladder in it hard up against the pipes carrying steam for the engines that pumped the water out. It was a long, long climb. Anyone who had tried it, and they would have to have been young and fit, had come out soaked with sweat and exhausted. And the road that connected Mauricewood to Greenlaw was way above the main workings. But still, I wasn't the only one that prayed that there would be a stream of them stumbling out and looking for us when we got to the pithead.

I was halfway up the hill when the mother of one of the boys in the cart ran down towards us. We'd heard screams when we were at the foot of the brae – that must have been when they told her. She'd come up to the pit from another direction. We all stopped as she went by. We could scarce bear the look on her face. She was running so fast that she tripped and fell. As someone lifted her up, she grabbed hold of them and shouted her child's name. Had they seen him? When they said yes, and she could see the pity in their face, she shut her eyes, holding her breath till she gathered her skirt about her, wiped the blood that trickled down her cheek and set off again down the brae. I looked back after a few steps and saw two women emerge from the crowd, put their arms round her and hurry off.

The pithead was swarming with people when we got there, mostly women, some with children, older men with sons down the pit, men that weren't on shift that day turning up to see if they could help, everyone wanting to know what was going on, who'd got out, how many were still down, what was being done to get them out. I found Sadie speaking to some of her neighbours. She had the baby with her. They were in a huddle beside the spoil heaps. The sieves that the sifters had been using earlier lay where they'd been flung down.

We'd get bits of the story. There were about sixty of them still down there. Of the two that had come up alive, one of them, Bill Robb the bottomer, was away back down again. Some said it was a bad conscience because he should have stayed where he was until all the men were counted out, and that he'd made sure of his own safety when he'd jumped into a carriage that was on its way up. He was the only one that got out from the deep workings. Poor man, he felt so bad about what people were saying in that first week that he put a letter in the paper to defend himself. He'd been in a fire before and he thought if he could get up quick enough he'd be able to get to water pumped down the shaft. That put a stop to a lot of the badmouthing that he got and, give him his due, he near spent himself in the rescue effort. He'd gone right back down at the start even though he'd been affected by the smoke. The other lad that got out, Willie Gall, the engineer, had climbed up the main incline and had just about had it by the time they got him. The boys at the dookhead heard his shouts and were able to haul him out. He was in a bad way to start with but the doctors were able to send him home later. His wife had a terrible job keeping him in his bed because he was so determined to get back down the pit to help.

All afternoon we waited. They were trying all sorts to damp down the fire because no-one could get down for the smoke and the heat. They had the big ventilator fan roaring and had carted in loads of canvas to block off half the incline so that they could clear the smoke easier but it was hard going. The men took it in turns to go down for as long as they could. Every now and then we'd see them come out gasping and filthy with smoke then go back in again after two or three minutes. They had no time to speak. Love, the manager, was down there directing the proceedings. He stayed down the pit all that day and all that night. He had his son, he was a manager at Greenlaw, and managers from other collieries, to help him. I'll bet he was a worried man. He would know right away what the chances were. He would know right away when he saw that smoke and where it was coming from that there was no chance. And knowing what happened after, at the Inquiry, I can just see that his mind would have been working overtime to cover his own back. The Inspectors never got down the mine before the Inquiry; he kept them in the office, had them make do with plans of the mine workings and one or two people telling their stories. That was a bloody disgrace: the whole thing, the Company getting off with it, the way they bullied widows and grieving mothers into not claiming against them for fear of losing their houses and their Fund money. No wonder the women gave him what for all those times they got together and went up to his office to see what he was doing about getting the bodies out. Sadie was one that was hard on him. She shoved him one time she was so angry. She made damned sure that he knew what we thought about him and his company and that we all knew damned fine that it was his fault that there had been no way out for them that worked down the pit. Six months the most of them lay down there. Six months we waited and no betterness at the end of it.

Later on, a wet, dense fog came down. What between that and the blue smoke belching out of the fan housing, braziers burning and the lamps at the pithead, it was like we were all going to hell. By teatime most folk had given up any hope. A lot of them had gone away home to wait for news or worse. Sadie was away. She'd gone to see to the girls. I'd said I'd stay a while and let her know if there was any news. Reporters from the big papers had turned up by then. The police were keeping us all back and they'd sent for soldiers from Glencorse. They must have been worried that we were going to riot. There had been a big commotion at another mine through the west when it had gone on fire. But we were far too worried to even think about that.

The main rescue effort was conducted from the dookhead, the junction of the main incline with a road driven approximately 300 yards from the foot of the vertical shaft and thus 84 fathoms below the surface. The angle of the incline followed that of the mineral strata – 50° at Mauricewood.

A fathom measures six feet – the span of a man's outstretched arms. The vertical shaft at Mauricewood measured 84 fathoms; equivalent to the length of approximately ninety-two men laid end to end. The 80 fathom enginehouse was 80 fathoms further down the steep incline, and the lowest workings another 80.

However, beyond the dookhead, the distances in fathoms measured the angled mineshaft: the incline. So, the 80 fathom engine house was 145 2/3 fathoms below ground (if measured vertically to the surface), equivalent to the length of approximately 160 men, and the lowest workings, 204 fathoms or approximately 220 men.

At this lowest level, workings went off East and West for over 200 fathoms. Even the men who worked them had difficulty explaining their layout. Two engines, one at 80 fathoms, the other at the bottom of the incline, worked eighteen hours a day pumping out the continually rising water.

1 2

The vertical shaft was rectangular and was divided by a wooden wall. One section measured 14'6" by 5'6" and was for downcast (fresh) air and contained two cages, each large enough to accommodate a coal hutch or a group of men. The other section acted as a spent air vent.

When they emerged from the cages, the men had to walk from the foot of the vertical shaft along an underground road to the dookhead. Here, carriages running on rails with a gauge of 3 feet 3½, which each held two hutches, ran all the way down the main incline.

The carriages were operated using 'dook' ropes which came from a separate enginehouse on the surface, and passed down the vertical shaft before branching off down the incline. The carriages could carry men or coal. As one ascended, the other descended under the control of a signalman at the dookhead.

1 2

The rescuers were led by Mr Love and his son – an underground manager at Greenlaw. Managers from neighbouring collieries, including Mr John Anderson of Lochgelly, formerly of Mauricewood, arrived in quick succession; while Mr A. W. Turnbull, able secretary and commercial manager of the Company, hardly ever left the ground.

In the immediate vicinity of the shafts stood groups of clergymen – Presbyterian, Episcopalian, and Roman Catholic – all forgetting their common differences in common sorrow, with some of the Directors of the Company, including Mr Carlow, Chairman of the Board; and numbers of men ready to relieve those who worked below.

Orders were given that the carriages be run constantly up and down so that any men who had been able to withstand the effects of the smoke and struggled to the foot of the incline would have some means of escape. But the incline was choked with smoke and fumes.

Only four, three boys and a man, managed to throw themselves into a carriage. Two of the boys were dead on arrival at the dookhead. The others showed some traces of life, but breathed their last when brought to the light. The bodies were somewhat bruised and marked by fire.

6

Drs W and R Badger, Dr Willis, Drs Riddell senior and junior, and Dr Anderson of the Glencorse Depot, were on the banks ready to give every assistance but all their skill was of no avail. The names of the three boys were Thomas Foster, Robert Tolmie, and George Pennycook.

The bodies were conveyed to Shottstown in carts just after two o'clock. Their blackened and distorted faces created a most painful sensation, and evoked much sympathy from the crowds they met on the way. Thomas Foster's face had been violently struck as the front of his skull was broken in.

It would be vain to attempt description of the scenes in the village. Many of the women ran off to the pithead when first the news of the disaster spread, and the dumb tearless eyes of some, equally with the uncontrolled weeping of others, were alike painful to the beholder.

But while many went to the scene, others stayed at home waiting in awful suspense to see whether those dear to them would return. Clergymen went from house to house administering the consolations of the gospel, doing their very best to prepare the bereaved for the determination of their uncertainty.

6

The relief party immediately saw the impossibility of passing the barrier of fire. They directed all their efforts to the construction of a canvas partition to obtain two passages: fresh air forced down one to force smoke out the other and clear the way for the rescuers to the bottom.

The Manager and other officials directed operations from the dookhead where cold water falling from above refreshed the atmosphere. They ran carriages into the heat and smoke of the incline, rescuers skilfully fixing, when they gained the limit of descent, props on which the canvas of the brattice was nailed.

For hours they laboured with this object, the monotonous alarm of the gong signalling the ascent and descent of the cage. Returning, deranged and stupefied by the hurried journey, the place of these earnest men was taken by others – four at a time – and thus the work was rapidly executed.

Mr A. W. Turnbull, Secretary of the Shotts Iron Company, was on the spot throughout yesterday, and the scene of the disaster was also visited by several of the Directors, among whom were Mr Bell of Cliftonhall, Chairman of the Company, Mr Jordan, and Mr James Thomson, ship owner, Leith.

6

They found Hugh McPherson and Jock Walker about midnight. They found them near the engine house. They'd been working with Willie Gall but neither of them was young and Jock Walker had a gammy leg. The smoke had overtaken them. Hugh was burnt bad and Jock's face was a mess of blood. I was away home by then. About seven o'clock word had come that the coal was on fire. And you could smell it. At first the smoke had smelt like a bonfire but it had turned more sulphurous and once you noticed it, you couldn't ignore it. That wasn't a good thing to know. If we'd been giving up hope before then, we knew that this was grim. There were some sobbing their hearts out but most just looked stunned, as if they didn't know what to do. We all knew that if the coal was on fire the only way it could be put out would be to pump water in till the flames died down and the last time that happened, when there was a small fire that had killed no one, it had taken four days to put out. So what between visions of them being roasted alive and the thought of them drowning everyone was about off their heads.

My sister, Chrissie, took me home then and stayed with me. I don't know how I ever slept and yet I was so exhausted I couldn't do anything but give in to it. All that was in my head was that as long as there was never a knock at the door there was still a chance, still a chance that Davie'd found somewhere away from the fire and they'd get to him. I didn't dare to think too much about the fire. Every now and then a thought would shoot through me and I'd let out a yelp. Chrissie cooried me in and lay beside me all night. When I woke and saw her face it took me a minute to remember what was going on. I'd been dreaming about Davie; he was behind a door but I couldn't get it open. Then the reality of it all came crashing in. I jumped out of the bed saying that I had to get up to the pit. I had to get up there to look for him. I had no time for a cup of tea. My poor sister, she tried to get me to stop a minute and gather myself together, to get something hot inside me but I was out the door with my shawl in my hand, my boots scarce buttoned.

The mist still hung in the air and I was sure that I could smell smoke in it. I looked up the road to Mauricewood but it was too thick to see anything. Chrissie came out behind me and shut the door. There were lights on in a good few houses round about. I wondered if they'd found any more bodies through the night. Chrissie said that you didn't know whether to hope that they had or not. Just then the McPherson's door opened and Mr Crockett, the Minister from our Church, came out with two women I recognised from the Mission. We rushed across for we knew the McPhersons well, Hugh had worked beside our father for years when they were young. It was the Minister told us they'd found Hugh, along with Jock Walker. We asked about Peter, that was Hugh's son, and about the rest of them. Had they got any more out through the night? But the Minister and the two women with him shook their heads. No, they hadn't found Peter or anyone else yet, just those two and the four at the start. The women from the Mission had been up all night alongside the Minister seeing what was needed, sitting with those who waited. They looked exhausted. Mr Crockett told them that they should go home now and get some rest because they didn't know what was in front of them. Mr Crockett wasn't stuffy like some of the Ministers. There was always something going on at our church. We'd have socials and talks and people would come and speak to us about their missionary work (the Mission women were always raising money for converting the heathen), and we had some smashing days out. A big crowd of us would load up on horses and carts and away for the day to Peebles, or Musselburgh.

Chrissie hoo-hoo'd in at the McPherson's door. Their next-door neighbour appeared and said for us to come away in.

Isa, Hugh's wife, was through in the room. Hugh lay on the bed on top of an old sheet. The room stank of smoke but at the same time of cold damp. Hugh's clothes were black and so was he, not just the usual sooty black but oily, thick-looking black. Isa sat beside the bed, her face puffy with crying, a hanky twisted between her fingers. She rose to greet us and broke down when we put our arms around her. Oh, lassies, she said, how will I ever be right again? We cried along with her, asked about Peter, asked who she had to help her for Hugh would need dressed, asked what the Minister had said. They hadn't found Peter yet. They still hadn't managed to get to the foot of the incline. They wouldn't get anyone out till they could get down there but it didn't look good because the smoke was bad. I looked at Hugh lying there and I thought about Davie and the others, about how many of them would be leaving wives with children and how many of them were children themselves. And the feeling that came over me was so strong that if any of those who had to do with the Shotts Iron Company had been there, I'd not have been happy until I'd smashed their heads open on the stone floor.

We got Isa back into her chair and her neighbour brought a cup of tea. She offered us a cup and Chrissie said yes, we'd have one, because this one, nodding in my direction, had been in too much of a hurry when she got up that we'd had nothing. Isa took a sip of tea and told us that the Minister had been awful good. He'd said a comforting prayer and the women from the Mission that had come along with him were going to get mort cloths and other things for she'd nothing like that ready in the house. Well, there was a good nightshirt in the drawer that had never been on, that would maybe do, but they were fetching what she'd need. And she turned to Hugh, put the cup on the floor and never went back to it. She looked at his face and put her hand on his arm. He was going stiff already. She was worried that they might not be able to get his clothes off to get his body dressed. I said they could cut them off if they needed to, although his jacket and trousers were ragged as if the fire had caught him from the back. And did she want us to give her a hand? No, no, she would wait till the women from the Mission came back. They said they wouldn't be long. We got our cups of tea and I drank mine looking at Isa looking at Hugh, tears running down my face for her, for myself, for the whole thing.

William Gall was half stripped in the swelter of the engine house when his lamp failed in a rush of foul air. He belled for a carriage, but none came. He shouted to Walker and MacPherson to follow him up the incline, but he was hauled out alone near dead.

Walker and MacPherson had been repairing the eighty fathom pumping engine. Walker was lame. They were both over sixty. Around 4am on 6th September, the rescuers found their bodies on the incline nearby. Macpherson's was the first funeral. He was interred at Kirkhill with his son Peter who was seventeen.

At a service in the house before they buried the MacPhersons, the Minister read the 90th psalm. *Thou dost unto destruction man that is mortal turn... As with an overflowing flood, thou carriest them away... like the grass that grows at morn are they, cut down as even' doth fade.*

John Walker was a mechanical engineer who lived at James Place, Penicuik with his wife Elizabeth. His family were all grown up. He had been a much respected elder in the Parish Church for eight years and on the previous Monday had been made chairman of the Co-operative Association Committee.

1 2 6

Davie wasn't a miner, not in the way that some were in that it was in their families. He'd take a job down the pit if it was paying better and if there was no other work on the go. He'd been brought up on farms out by West Linton and had worked in the fields from when he was anything. He loved to be outside. When he was working down the pit, I've seen him out all night in the summer, fishing – there was always a bit of poaching going on – or he'd be away up hills or along the waterside with the dog. He loved his dog and it loved him. It pined away when he didn't come home.

He was down the pit when I first knew him. It was when Sadie first got together with Johnny Glass. Johnny was lodging with Davie and his first wife, Maggie. Not that I knew him then, just knew him through Sadie, through her telling me about the family; they only had Helen then. That was before Maggie died. Martha was born in the middle of January and by the October, Maggie was dead. Her kidneys packed in. She died in the Infirmary in Edinburgh.

His mother took the children to Innerleithen to live with her because he couldn't look after them and work. The poor things. She was a hard woman, Davie's mother. I never took to her. Davie reckoned something bad had happened to her; she couldn't sleep if she thought a window might be open but in the house, the room doors were never shut. An old farmhand who had worked near where she was brought up told him stories about a shepherd they called Creepin Tam. And I think that made him wonder and he let things go that he maybe wouldn't have otherwise. One of her favourite sayings was many's the devil that comes with a smiling face. I don't know if Davie's father had any idea. He always said she'd only married him because she couldn't face the embarrassment of her younger sister being married before her. I know she regretted not saying yes to the farmer's son who asked her because she cast that up when she was angry with him. And he'd say something like, well if you would favour looks over money there's nothing I can do about that.

Martha and Helen couldn't get away from their granny quick enough. I'd have taken them gladly but she wasn't for letting them go. They were too much use to her – little more than skivvies. I told Davie that, but his mother could always soft soap him, and well, his father was very fond of them and they'd never really known any different, that was their home. But I'll tell you now, if I'd known, if Davie had known, just what would happen to them after he died, he'd have had them out of there as quick as wink. I offered to take them with me to Edinburgh when I had to get out of the house because it belonged to the Company. I'd got the chance of a good job there. It was a live-in position and the girls could have been in a grand house but if they went, their granny would lose out on the Fund money that belonged to them. Not that they saw much of it from what Martha told me later on. Her and Helen weren't even allowed up to the table to eat their dinner. It was as if Davie dying ratcheted up his mother's bad temper till she lost herself in it. And as each of them got to be fourteen and the Fund stopped that was them out to work. Both of them into the mill. Helen, she got away to be married and went down to Ashington. And Martha, she got away when she went up to Edinburgh to work for Mr Henry Dobson, the painter. He was from Innerleithen and was doing well by then. He took Martha in to help his wife about the house, to help with his children. The Dobsons were good to her, treated her a sight better than she was used to that's for sure. Their youngest boy, Cowan, he ended up an artist too, he fairly took to her, called her Atta because he couldn't say Martha. She had a beautiful complexion, Martha. Henry Dobson put her into some of his paintings on account of it. I saw one once, in a shop window in Edinburgh. I recognised her straight away. She was pouring a saucer of milk for a cat.

It says a lot for those two girls how they turned out. Both ended up married to decent men and with families of their own. They had great spirit the pair of them, never let things get them down. Hard-working girls too, both quiet like their mother but both full of fun when they got the chance. Martha loved to sing and dance, and Helen was never happier than when she was looking after something. She'd play for hours with cats or dogs or bairns. But when she lost her Dad she would hardly speak to anybody. And nervous? She even started wetting the bed. That didn't go down too well with Davie's mother.

They doted on their dad. Not that they saw him very often, or me either, but when they did, they just about ate us they were so pleased to see us. And we'd always have something for them, even if it was just a sweetie. But if they needed anything expensive, like shoes or coats, Davie would give his mother the money. And the two of them could wind him round their little fingers. I'll never forget the time he bought Martha a pair of buttoning boots. She'd been so desperate for a pair of those boots: the kind that come up over the ankle and fasten up the front with a hook. She was so excited when we brought them. I'd got them at the Store in Penicuik: soft black leather with mother-of-pearl buttons. You would have thought that all her birthdays had come at once. She had to get them on right there and then and she would have been in her bed with them on if we'd let her. She was wearing them when his mother brought her and Helen up to see the big funerals on the Sunday.

Between five and six o'clock, two of Her Majesty's Inspectors of Mines arrived and at once descended the shaft. The wooden linings and ladders of the upset and dook were on fire but then the character of the smoke changed. The Penicuik gas manager confirmed that coal must be burning.

Mr Anderson attempted to get beyond the seat of the fire by a semi-circular passage leading past the stables. He made short progress when his light was extinguished by black damp but not before he saw flasks lying on the ground thrown down by those who had fled the fire.

Rescuers tried to douse flames in the east side but the heat was too intense. The pumping engines had been destroyed. The roof dropped in detached masses around them. They waded knee-deep in the black, reeking flood, while beyond the fire leapt and raved, bodies visible in the red glow.

They found six bodies on an elevated platform above the waist-deep water, clustered together as they had lain themselves down to die. They floated the dead on hastily made rafts and sent them up to the bereaved who waited amidst clouds of foul-smelling smoke scattered abroad by the incessant fan.

6

The dread harvest of death was gathered slowly but surely. The rumble of the carts as they went forward conveying the remains of the miners begot a feeling of shuddering awe which will not easily be forgotten by those who witnessed the painful procession to this door, and the other.

The dead carts rumbled along the dusty ways, and the multitude of women, till now restrained, fell upon the wagons crying aloud for their murdered husbands. Ministers calmed the women; reverently they laid aside the face-cloths, no better than rough sacking, identified the poor mishandled clay, and accompanied them home.

Not a few painful incidents could be told of the sickening despair evinced as the bereaved listened in the stillness of the night for the noise of the carts or in the daytime looked out along the road, not knowing to whose door the dread vehicles might next be directed.

Little ceremony was indulged in. Remains were placed in carts as they left the pit. The carriers announced the names of the deceased, and the women gave way to unrestrained lamentations. With great tenderness, corpses were carried into the houses, shoulders and heads covered with canvas bags, faces occasionally seen.

6 3

We'd had a taste of what was coming on the Saturday when they'd buried Hugh and Peter McPherson. The Minister, Mr Jamieson of the Parish Church, conducted a service in the house. They'd moved the coffins out to give people room and they were next door at the Wallace's. That was where the young girl drank the carbolic. I went with my sister Chrissie. I'll never forget the look on Isa's face when it came time to leave for the cemetery. I thought she's not going to be able to bury them. She shut her eyes and just kind of folded into the shoulder of her older son. I knew they'd had to tear her away from Peter's coffin. They needed to nail the lid shut and she kept saying just another minute, just another minute, I'm not ready to leave him just yet. Then she'd stroked his face and said night, night son. Betty Wallace could hardly speak when she told me about it. But then Isa gathered strength from somewhere and she walked that road up the Kirkhill and never took her eyes off the two coffins in front of her. It was as if she never saw the hundreds of people that had come to see the funeral. Old Colonel Borthwick and his deputy were ordering the police about, making sure they kept the crowd in order, and there were soldiers on the gate at the new cemetery – soldiers – I don't know what they thought we were going to do.

But oh, the sight that met us. Heaps of dirt everywhere where they'd been digging graves for all those who were to be buried on the Sunday. It took our breath away – so many – and from the size of the heaps of dirt, we could see that there were going to be more than one in some of the holes. They were so deep they had ladders in them. I tried my best to concentrate on what the Minister was saying, on singing the hymns, on keeping my eyes closed tight during the prayers, not to get overwhelmed at the thought of all that death still waiting for us, not to think about what was going on across the valley at Mauricewood.

I'd noticed, and two or three other people had said, that

there didn't seem to be so much smoke coming from the direction of the pit but it was hard to see as it was still misty. We all knew that the fire wasn't out and from what they said, it would take more than a few days to damp it down with water. But if we'd known what was going on, those police and those soldiers would have had their hands full. There would have been a riot. While we were burying Hugh and Peter McPherson they were capping the mine, sealing it with concrete so that no air could get in to feed the fire. No air could get into anyone that was still alive down there either, and what nobody knew then was that there were people still alive, and not just a handful. That was obvious when they got to them in the March. They found a crowd of them behind a stopping four feet thick. And they hadn't died quickly. One of them, Tom Meikle, had had the time to scratch a message on his flask; you could hardly make it out but it was there. Davie was one of those that they didn't get out until the March. They reckon that George Muir, the oversman, had taken a group of those that were fit and able and tried to get out another way as he would know all the workings like the back of his hand. But they had no chance, for even if they had got back to the incline, there was no way up because it was on fire; from the minute he was checked at the engine house, he must have known that their case was hopeless.

We didn't know all this when we were standing on the Kirkhill. All we knew was that there were more than twenty-two to bury the next day. The Ministers had organised Church services for them and we were all going.

The decision to seal the pit was made on Saturday by the Inspector of Mines, Mr Love the pit manager, and the Shotts Iron Company. The pit was closed with battens of wood covered with clay. Forty families had lost a father or son and 160 children were left fatherless.

On Saturday, ninth September, Mr Love, the mine manager, issued a statement to the press in which he denied that there had been any breach of the Regulations, and in particular stressed that there were two means of exit from the lower working as required by statute. Not everyone agreed.

On 6 September the TUC, meeting in Dundee, requested that the government institute an open enquiry into an apparent contravention of the Acts of Parliament. There were two shafts in Mauricewood, but one of these might have been placed at the Rock of Gibraltar for all the good it did.

It is understood that communications have been opened with the Lord Provost of Edinburgh by the Directors of the Company with the view of raising a subscription for the dependents of those who have lost their lives in the Disaster. The Shotts Iron Company has promised a donation of £500.

6

I've never seen anything like that Sunday. People had come from all over. From first thing they'd turned up in fancy jaunting cars, on horseback, on foot; the street along from us was lined with horses and carts. A lot of strangers went to the morning services. I had no time to go to the Church that morning because Davie's mother and the two girls were coming up in the train and I had to feed them. I'd said to Sadie just to come too so that the girls could be company for one another. My mother and Chrissie helped me. My mother brought a stew and Chrissie had made a gingerbread. I managed to gather myself together enough to make a pot of soup and boil some potatoes. But my head wasn't in the right place. I had no carrots for the soup so I'd put some beetroot in and it turned out a hell of a colour, and there was no salt in the potatoes. But nobody seemed to notice. Helen and Martha tucked in like they'd hardly been fed for a week and it was only after, when I thought about it, that I realised that maybe they hadn't. They'd been pretty quiet when I met them off the train. Davie's mother was grey. I never thought I'd see this day she said. And I had to make it worse for her. I had to tell her that they'd capped the pit.

On Sunday morning many strangers visited the pithead. A strong force of police were noticed in one of the colliery buildings, and the tent erected for the accommodation of the military still stood, but that was all there was left to gratify the curiosity of any who visited the scene.

The Salvation Army held a service in the street which was respectfully listened to by many of the strangers who were beginning to make their appearance. The voice of the young woman who spoke thrilled with emotion as she pointed upwards and told of One who could do all that they required.

Numbers of strangers had sought admission to the churches in the forenoon. At the Established Church, before taking their seats, many had made a circuit of the open graves in the churchyard behind, and had brought home to their minds the results of the Disaster and their own inevitable mortality.

6

In the Free Church, Rev. Crockett spoke the words in Romans xii.15 – "weep with them that weep:" With the printed list of the dead held in his hand as the emblem of a world of desperate grief and grim suffering, he enforced the lessons to be gathered from the Disaster.

...would there be not some good fruit from that bitter flower if the law became so strict that nevermore would more than half a hundred men be left to die with no chance of escape, without even a poor man's consolation of fight for life and wife and little ones?

If the disaster did nothing else, it should make the inspection of mines more frequent and real, questions would surely be asked in the highest councils of the nation. Looking to spiritual issues, already many obdurate hearts desirous of knowing the better way of life had turned to the Lord.

The Free Church dates from 1843, when one third of ministers split from the Established Church. Congregations wanted to be free to appoint their own ministers, to be free from state interference or patronage. In this, the Free Church stands in direct line with the Reformation and the National Covenants.

6 15

When Davie's mother saw all the people who had come to see the funerals, she could scarce believe it. She didn't have a good word to say about any of them. I can't remember what word she used, it wasn't vultures, but it wasn't flattering. Mind you, she wasn't far wrong, a good lot of them were there because they were heart sorry for us and at what had happened, but there were a good few that were there to get their fill of our misery. They'd been up at the pit and round the graveyards; they were the ones that weren't too pleased when the hotel had to shut because it had run out of drink. The police had to chase them before things got out of hand. The papers said there were about sixteen thousand people in Penicuik that day, and it felt like it. They were about ten deep along the streets and there was such a crowd in the Square that the cortege could hardly get round the corner to go up the Kirkhill. There were soldiers at the sides of the roads. They were at the gravesides too to make sure the families got some peace.

We didn't go up to the Kirkhill. We went back to the house and stood at the back door because we could see the cemetery from there. We'd gone to the Church, Davie's mother was determined she was getting inside to hear the service but we stayed outside with the children. Mr Crockett spoke to the thousands gathered outside. Nothing like the sermon he'd given earlier though seemingly. He'd been on his high horse at the morning service, waving a sheet of paper in the air with all the names of the dead, and spouting off against the Company and the Mines Inspectors for there being no way out for those who were trapped. He hadn't minced his words; two days later he got a letter from the Company's solicitors threatening libel. But at the funerals, he kept it simple, he wouldn't want to be disrespectful.

There were fourteen coffins lined up on the gravel outside the doors of the United Presbyterian Church. Lads from the Volunteers and a squad of miners all dressed in black had brought the most of them. They'd carried them on long white poles. Two or three they'd taken out of some houses, and not a few of those had had to come out through the windows because that was easier.

Davie's mother had a good nose at the coffins before she went in to the Church. She looked like a crow with her mourning clothes on and that sharp face. Each coffin had a name and the date of the Disaster on a brass plate. We knew them all. There was Alex McKinlay, he left five of a family, although the youngest one died just not long after. The boy Sommerville that had been taken to the wrong house because they didn't recognise him. Jock Walker that they'd found with Hugh McPherson: he was an elder of the Kirk and was on the Store committee. And at least two lots of brothers: the Wrights who had another brother still lost down the pit, and the Wallaces, Andrew just fourteen.

The principal funeral service was conducted at the United Presbyterian Church, the majority of the deceased being Presbyterians. Fourteen coffins were brought to the church door where they were laid on a double row of benches on the gravel walk inside the railings on either side of the main door.

The Rev. Thomson preached from second Corinthians – "We walk by faith and not by sight." He sought to give comfort and proceeded to tell how *the heart of Shottstown this day is raw and bleeding. Words from human lips seem mockery – an insult in the ears of such bitter affliction.*

Rev. McKerrow preached from Isaiah xxvi.9, *With my soul have I desired thee in the night.* His sermon told of the painful vision of the doomed men brought face-to-face with death, forced by the stifling smoke to realise their inevitable fate, and of the unavailing struggle with their pitiless enemy.

Ibid. 10: Let favour be shewed to the wicked, *yet* will he not learn righteousness: in the land of uprightness, will he deal unjustly.
21: The Lord cometh to punish the inhabitants of the earth for their iniquity: the earth shall disclose her blood, and no more cover her slain.

1 6 13

At the Catholic Church, Father McAnaa's text was, "It is appointed unto men once to die", from Paul's letter to the Hebrews. He proclaimed that *until the village ceased to be, there was no doubt that the disaster of 5th September would wander weirdly through the memories of the people.*

Aged men would tell of the message from the burning mine which told the child, "Your father is no more;" the mother, "Your child is dead;" and the wife, "Your husband lies deep and dead in the earth." Thus the voice of God bids us prepare for our coming death.

That message had now reached every dwelling in the land, and was known beyond the seas and the mountains. *But we are not parted from our brethren. Chains of the communion of saints bind us – draw us around God's throne to praise him for this exhibition of his divine teaching.*

We praise him for having in his wisdom taken out of our midst this boy Sinnet whose body has so often been sanctified by the blood of Christ at these altar rails. We weep for the departed, and with bowed hearts take from God's hands this lesson and this warning.

6

On Friday, 6th September, a little after one, three sonorous strokes of the gong betokened the ascent of the cage. It brought up the body of John Sinnet. He was found lying over a carriage at the foot of the incline just beyond a dead pony, his face badly burned.

On the day of the Disaster, John Sinnet, fan-keeper, was working only his third shift down the mine. He was fifteen and a bright lad, but his mother was in a lunatic asylum and his father didn't make much as a cattleman and there were four other mouths to feed.

He was the only Catholic among the dead. His coffin was placed on a catafalque erected in front of the altar rails. Its mourning pall of black velvet was smothered in wreaths of white flowers. Candles burned on either side; the chapel was crowded. Two priests attended at the graveside.

1 2 6

Then, after the service, we had to wait for Davie's mother to come out of the Church. We'd said that we'd wait across the road near the Store. That wasn't such a good idea. There were so many people, and with all the hearses being loaded up and soldiers not allowing people to cross the street while they organised the procession, we thought we'd lost her; not that that would have been a bad thing. But then she appeared with a soldier in tow. She'd given him such a big sob story about her son lost down the pit and his widow and children waiting for her across the street that he'd escorted her across the road himself.

The procession was huge. The Volunteers were at the front, then the Ministers – the Presbyterians went first, then the Catholics, then the Episcopalians from the English Kirk. The English Kirk minister and the priests had their fancy robes on. There were more priests than Catholics to bury. Just the boy Sinnet who'd only been down the pit three days. They said he was a bright boy but his family needed the money so he went to work and that was that. It was a terrible shame though, he was only fifteen. The chapel had been full for his funeral mass. They'd taken him there earlier that morning. The poor lad, there was only his father and his sister there to bury him from his family. His mother was in the asylum.

And there were only three to bury from the English Kirk. There was Tommy Adams who lived just a few doors along from us in Manderston Place. His wife, Andrina, was left with two wee girls, one just weeks old. There was the boy Urquhart from the station at Eskbridge, and another, I can't remember his name, his mother was a widow and his pay was what kept them. I remember they lived in Napier Street. Frizell was it not? No, Fraser, that was it, the boy Fraser; his nephew ran the paper.

Then came Love the manager with a toff that we didn't recognise. He was tall and thin – long as a fathom of pump water as my mother would have said. When the whisper went round that he was one of the heads of the Company, a chill ran through me. I couldn't help but think that between them, him and Love, and whoever else had to do with the running of the pit, had killed my Davie. I couldn't help but notice his top hat and the fine cut of his clothes. I said as much to Sadie, and I wasn't the only one saying it. I like to think that he didn't look comfortable but I don't know. Love looked pretty haggard, haunted even. Well I hope that the sound of those hearses behind him haunted his every step.

A crowd of mourners followed them: local bigwigs and those as always put themselves forward for those kinds of things, then the Boys Brigade. And the Salvation Army, they had to get their noses in. They were near the back, just in front of the Royal Scots. We were never stuck for a soldier in Penicuik with the barracks just along the road at Glencorse. Young George Pennycook had been in the Boys Brigade, he'd only be fourteen. They'd got some of the lads to bring him to the Mission Hall where they'd laid his cap and his belt on top of the coffin. I remember Jean Smith telling me that his sister had been inconsolable at the graveside. People had felt so sorry for her that they'd given her the cap and belt to keep. Jean said the poor girl had cuddled them in tight and cried so hard they almost had to carry her away.

They'd had to get hearses from all round about, even from Edinburgh, and oh, they were beautiful: the horses with their black ostrich plumes, every coffin covered in the most beautiful wreaths. The Misses Cowan had sent a wreath to every one of those who had died and they did the same again come the Spring when we buried the rest of them. People don't forget those kinds of things. Behind each hearse came the mourners. You could hear the sobs of the crowd above the sound of the horses' feet and the rolling of the hearse wheels on the road. And there was a strong smell of horse dung with there being so many of them. Davie would have been wanting to be out there with a pail and a shovel collecting it once it was all over. Not that we had a garden at Manderston Place, none of us did, they built them without gardens so that you had to buy everything. But my mother had a garden and Davie kept it tidy for her – grew tatties and vegetables. He liked the garden and he always liked to have plenty dung on it. Many's the time we'd be out gathering sheeps droppings; tottles he called them or shairney. That was one of his jokes; he'd ask you a question then when you answered he'd say are you shairney, making it sound more like are you sure now, and if you said yes, well you'd fallen for it.

At the Kirkhill, an immense grave had been dug in common ground. Interred there were George Livingstone, 45; David Wallace, 22, and his younger brother Andrew Falconer Wallace, 14; their brother-in-law, Alexander Kerr McKinley, 28; Thomas Adams, 24; William Urquhart, 18; and John Fraser, 16. These last three were Episcopalians.

George (Doddie) Livingstone was forty-five and single. Well known in Midlothian quoiting circles, he lived at Fieldsend with his eighty-four-year-old mother, Mrs. Magdalene Livingstone, who had worked in the pits when she was nine. She was failing. He had been successful at the sports held the weekend before the Disaster.

The coffins of Andrew Falconer Wallace who was thirteen and his brother David who was twenty-two were two of the fourteen laid on the gravel outside the church. Andrew was a member of the Boy's Brigade. David had been on nights but had changed shifts that day with Harry Hope.

Alexander Kerr McKinley, a miner, was twenty-eight. His wife was three months pregnant with their fourth child. They had a son aged five and a daughter aged three. Their youngest, Alex, was ten months old. He died on November 16th, 1889. His brother, William, was born on 7th March, 1890.

1 6

The Episcopalians had been given use of the schoolroom in the Free Church Hall at Fieldsend for their funeral service. The three coffins were laid on a table that was covered in a white cloth. They contained the remains of Thomas Adams and two boys: William Urquhart and John Fraser.

Thomas Adams was twenty-four. His widow, Andrina, was left with two children, one aged two years and one aged two months. William Urquhart was eighteen and lived at Eskbridge station. His father would be completely overcome at the graveside. John Fraser had been the sole support of his widowed mother.

Several wreaths lay on each coffin. Three more were added while the mourners awaited the Reverends Thomson and Erlington. These were from Lady and Miss Clerk who were present at the service which was led by the choir of St. James the Less, Penicuik and the choirboys of Roslin Chapel.

1

The mourning card for Robert Hunter told that he was the beloved husband of Margaret Learmonth, and showed the outline of a mausoleum over which two angels sounded the final trumpet. When they recovered his body he had clawed his fingers to the bone in his efforts to get out.

Learmonth is an ancient Scottish surname. Historically associated with the eastern Tweed basin, it has a French origin that implies the merging of two glittering streams. Thomas the Rhymer was a member of this ancient family, as was the Russian poet, Lermontov. Learmonths were pioneer settlers in the New World.

Robert Hunter had five children, the youngest born Christmas Eve, 1889. Verses on his mourning card included the lines: *Wrapped in thy shroud, in that deep sleep, When we did touch thy face so pale, Dear loved one it did make us weep, But what could all our tears avail.*

1 15

When the procession was past, we went back to the house and had a cup of tea. We stood out at the back door because you could see the Kirkhill from there and watched as the crowd split up and spread out round the graves, as the Ministers and priests held their hands in the air for the blessings. We heard the sound of bagpipes and voices singing. We couldn't quite make out the tunes because we just got snatches of it when there was a loud bit. I was sure I could hear Mr Crockett; he had such a strong voice and would be leading whatever singing was going on. His wife was a lovely singer too, always sung solo at the church socials.

All our speaking was to do with what we'd seen, what the services had been like, what time Davie's mother and the girls would get back down the road because they didn't want to be late home for Davie's father and, well, the girls would be needing their beds; it had been a long day. Nothing was said about Davie being lost or about how that made any of us feel. Maybe it was because the girls were there and that might have upset them too much. But I think it was more that we didn't dare; it would have been too much to cope with.

The girls were quiet but then they always were when their granny was there. The wee smouts, I made sure they got an extra slice of gingerbread with their tea and wrapped some up for them to take home.

It's a wonder they didn't miss the train. There were so many people milling around the town, and some of them in none too good a mood with the hotel having run out of beer by dinnertime. But we joined the crowd heading for the station and were there in plenty time. You'll let us know if they find him was about as much as Davie's mother said. The girls gripped my skirt. Helen asked me if I would still come and see them even if they didn't find her Dad, and Martha said Jesus'll find him because she'd been praying every night. I waved them off and my heart fair burst. I walked through crowds of strangers with tears soaking my face and the breath hiccupping out of me. It wasn't as if I would be an uncommon sight that day. You could see that people were sympathetic, they stood back to let me past. I was meant to be going to Sadie's, but I couldn't think to be with people right then. I couldn't think what to do with myself. Next thing I knew I'd pushed my way into the old cemetery. There were a few people there looking at the fresh graves and so I didn't feel out of place. This was where Davie would be buried when we found him. Maggie was in there underneath a big tree against the back wall but there was no headstone. I went to where I was sure she was and I spoke to her. I told her he was lost and hadn't been found yet but I'd make sure that he was and that he got a good burial. And I said I'd seen the girls and how bonny they both were, how loving. I didn't tell her what I thought of Davie's mother. I told her not to worry about them; as long as I was working I'd be able to put a coat on their backs. I said how lucky we both were to have known Davie and that he had never stopped loving her. I'd known that from the start. But I knew how much he loved me for myself, and, if I ever felt jealous, all I did was remind myself that Maggie was dead.

I sat down on the grass and looked at the ruins of the old Kirk with its steeple starting to crumble, at the graves fresh covered with flowers from earlier in the day and I was past tears. All that came out of me was a kind of moan and my insides heaved about like a heavy sea. I wandered across to one of the fresh graves. Trees made it darker down there and, over the railings, the ground dropped away to the Valleyfield Mill. From the wreaths, I realised that this was where they'd buried Martin Stark and his nephew that morning. I couldn't think that Martin was dead. In my mind I could still see him when we were young and daft. There was a time when all he would have had to do was ask me and I'd have been his, but he never saw me that way; he was always friendly, but he only had eyes for the lass he married. And I thought of her left with a baby to bring up by herself and it just months old. Well that was me in tears again. Then I smiled to myself when I realised that I was right up against the railings of one of the posh graves. It was a Thorburn or a Brown of Esk Mill. The thought of all the people that would have been clambering on their fancy ironwork and nothing they could do about it lightened my spirits enough to get me out of there and along the road to Sadie's.

The town stank of horses, horses and the smells of people in their Sunday best that had been on the go all day – sweat and mothballs and every now and then the whiff of whisky or cigars. Some of the hearses were going up the street on their way back to wherever they had come from for the day. Their drivers pushed the horses on at a fair lick, they'd be keen to get home. It made me wonder about the poor animals that were down the pit. I hoped they hadn't suffered too much. They'd had three ponies down there. There had been a right carry on when they took them down. That was the barely two years before the Disaster. They could get stuff out quicker because it meant that both miners in a pair could work at the face. So the Company had done the usual, dropped the price they paid the men for the coal and it ended up in a lockout for two months and still they had to take the cut. They got a fraction off their rent in compensation but the buggers just cut the price again and laid about fifty of them off. We thought Davie was lucky not to be one of them for he was on the ironstone and that was where the layoffs were. I wished he had been. He could have been back in the mill. He would have got a job no bother. He was working there when we got married but the money wasn't too good, and with him having the two girls to think about he had to go where the money was.

Mauricewood was not well unionised. In August 1886 the workers had had to accept a wages cut of 20%, while during December 1887 they were locked out for eight weeks and forced to take a cut of 1/- a ton after the introduction of ponies had brought about increased productivity.

Men would be laid off at a minute's notice if trade was slack; in May 1889 fifty were dismissed and the rest forced to take a cut in pay. In August 1889 the London dockers' strike gave the miners a good example of what could be achieved by workers' solidarity.

After the Disaster, the men turned to the Miners' Federation for help. Unfortunately, at that time it lacked the unity and economic strength required to champion their cause. The more radical union leaders, like Keir Hardie, were now advocating that the unions should support their own independent representatives of labour.

Gladstone supported the London dockers in their victorious strike of August 1889. He described it as 'a real social advance that tended to a fair principle of the division of profit' in a speech that was described as having no parallel except in the rhetoric of the toughest socialist leaders.

2 10

When I got to Sadie's her girls were supping glasses of milk and eating a slice of bread each. Sadie's mother was there stirring a pot on the fire. She was making soup for them for the next day. Aye, I'll burn in hell for working on a Sunday. But she wouldn't because she was a good, kind woman, Sadie's mother. There was some potted head on a plate on the table and the bread and two plates. Sadie's mother asked if that was them away. I said aye, but that I was worried for Helen and Martha, they'd taken it hard and Davie's mother was such a dour besom. Sadie came through from the back. She'd been filling the coal scuttle. She wondered where I'd been, if the train had been late away with all the commotion. So, I told her how I'd ended up at the Old Kirkyard because I'd got myself so upset at the thought of Martha and Helen with no father or mother and left with their granny. Sadie put the scuttle down beside the fire, wiped her hands and came across and gave me a cuddle for I was crying again. Aye, it's terrible, she said, but what can you do. What can any of us do just now? And she sat me down at the table and cut some bread. Not that either of us were hungry.

Once the girls were in their beds and her mother was away home, we blethered for a good while. I told Sadie how my insides welled up every time I thought about Davie being dead, and how it was like a screaming in my head, a terrifying, panicky feeling every time I wondered what had happened to him. And Sadie looked lost and said that she was doing things but she didn't know how because her every thought was with Johnny. Where was he? What had happened to him? And even though she knew that there was very little chance of him still being alive, there was a bit of her that hoped against hope that he'd found a safe hole somewhere and would still be there when they opened the pit again. I said oh, I know, because I wanted the same. But they'd capped it; shut it up good and tight with no word to anybody about how long it might stay like that, how long it might be before they opened it up again, and none of us could ever feel as if we'd done our best until the men were out of there. Sadie got herself so wound up about it that she made up her mind to go up to the Company offices in the morning to see what Love was doing about it, to demand that the Company get them out. I said to her that she'd maybe better take a few others with her; Love might get more of a fright if a crowd turned up. I couldn't go for I'd have to go back to work in the morning if I wanted to still have a job. So she said she'd see who she could organise to go with her. Good job I've not got a gun she said because I'd take it with me.

And that's what she did, gathered together a crowd of women that still had no bodies to bury and went up to Love's office. There were about forty they reckoned, some of them with children in tow. They shoved their way in and demanded that the Company get their men and their sons out of that hellhole. According to Love that was impossible because the pit was still on fire and they'd need to get the all-clear from them as knew about these things before they could open it up again. Well, that just riled the women. Sadie couldn't help herself. She shoved him and shouted that he'd managed to shut it up well enough himself, and another shoved him in the other direction shouting that there was no road for the men to come up, and Love said that there was as far as the law was concerned, and the one that had just shoved him the second time screamed into his face yes, there was a road, but what kind of road was it. Her brother had come up it once and it was like as though he'd been through a river he'd sweated so much. How could they be expected to climb all that way between hot steam pipes?

Well, the women got themselves in the paper for all the good it did them. The pit was opened again early in the October but by then it was flooded and no work could start until they got rid of the water. They never even started until the November. The women had been back at the office at least once before that creating a fuss, agitating for them to get a move on and get the mine cleared. Two months they were told it would take. Well they never got near a body till the end of the next March. All that winter if you went outside you'd hear the booming of the pumping engine and at the least strange noise, you'd be up at the window wondering if it was someone coming to say that they'd found them. It wasn't so bad for me in some ways because I had my work; and although I knew I'd have to get out of the house somewhere down the line, at least I had money coming in. For those with children or for those whose sons were dead and who'd been the bread winner, well, you can only imagine. The Company paid for the funerals and there was the Fund right enough but that didn't start right away. And even then, most of them would be lucky if half of it paid the rent. Mr Cowan, my boss at the paper mill and who was on the Fund Committee, had told them they could afford to be more generous. But oh no, they didn't dare give out more than looked careful. Some of the men had small insurances or were in the Co-op but even so, some of the families that were left must have been in debt and living in fear of the poor house. If it wasn't for the Fund, question how many of them would have ended up there. People sent money from all over the country, from abroad too, some even came from Russia, from miners there. The paper mill workers set aside a day's pay. And the local mining communities – well, I don't know how they did it – huge amounts they collected among themselves. They reckoned that the miners at Newbattle alone put more in than the Marquis of Lothian. Queen Victoria sent a telegram. And Mr Gladstone, our MP, not that he had much to do with the place, sent a letter via his wife to Mr Cowan at Beeslack, who was big in the local Liberal party, sending their condolences. They were in Paris when the Disaster happened, at the Exhibition. Mr Crockett, the Minister, had been there too, earlier in the week, preaching. He didn't have much to say that was good about the place or the Parisians. Pleasure seemed to be their God. Sundays were given over to cavorting, and gambling seemed to be a favourite pastime especially with the women. One had shot herself at the races when her horse fell. As far as he was concerned, they were all going to hell on the back of their useless Tower of Babel.

There were some as said Gladstone should have had a lot more to do with chasing the Company but he was too taken up with goings on in Ireland, Home Rule and the like – at least that was the impression folk got from the papers. Because the Company got off with the lot at the first Inquiry, a rap on the knuckles about a door hinge not being right but let right off the hook about there not being a road out. People were angry but not surprised at them getting off with murder, because that's what it was. As long as the money kept coming to line their pockets they weren't bothered how it got there. December was far too early anyway to have an Inquiry. How could they possibly know what had happened when they never got down there to look? I don't know how any of them that ran that company ever slept at night. £500 they put into the Fund. By the time the committee stopped taking donations it was over £20,000. The men who spoke for the miners at the Inquiry saw the Company's balance sheet for that year and they'd put down the money that they'd lost first before they mentioned how many had been killed. That's how those kinds of people think.

Mr Crockett was appointed to preach in Paris during the Exhibition where he was shocked by the utter disregard of the name of God. *He who pitied Jerusalem would also pity Paris with its Jacob's ladder – a useless structure of iron – pointing in the direction where their thoughts were not.*

Gladstone was in Paris from 3 to 9 September, 1889. On the fifth, he wrote letters in the morning, spent the forenoon at the Exhibition, dined at Saphiers then on to the Hippodrome where he was impressed by the cycling and the Russian spectacle. He also finished his latest manuscript.

On the sixth, Gladstone went early to the Exhibition. At the Indian Court he received beautiful & costly gifts. Later he saw examples of the old coal mine and the new. At night he went to the Opera. He sat in the President's box and was shown behind the scenes.

On Saturday, seventh September, after nine letters written, the Gladstones were again at the Exhibition. They were received most kindly by M. Eiffel & his coadjutors & Mr Gladstone was persuaded to go up the tower & propose his health in a French oratiuncle. Catherine was unhappily prevented by indisposition.

6 9

Sunday was the twelfth after Trinity. Gladstone went to church in the Rue d'Aguesseau both morning and afternoon then he and his wife drove to the Bois de Boulogne. Later they observed the illumination of the Eiffel Tower. He read Elizabethan Church History, Machale's *Letters* and *Crookleigh, a Village Story*.

In Paris, Mrs Gladstone took up her husband's pen to relate the grief the terrible accident at Mauricewood had given him. She asked Mr Cowan to make her husband's sympathy known and for information about the public fund as he was anxious to do something to help the poor sufferers.

On Monday, after writing letters and amid many kind farewells, the Gladstones returned to London, arriving at 6.30. They dined at Mr Hankey's. They saw various people and later Gladstone read the Orleans Letters and Dostoevsky's *Le Crime et le Châtiment*. They would head home to Hawarden in the morning.

After drinking brandy, Raskolnikov falls asleep on the grass and dreams of an incident from his childhood in which a group of peasants take cruel delight in beating an old mare to death. A young boy cries out against the act and nestles the dead mare's head in his arms.

9 14

The Company presented memorial scrolls to those who died or helped in the rescue. To the left of the dedication was an image of Mauricewood, the Pentlands behind, smoke blowing north-eastwards. *In Memoriam 5th September 1889* was inscribed on an escutcheon surrounded by fern leaves and an arc of snowdrops.

The Directors of The Shotts Iron Company desire to express to you, Mr Henry Love, Oversman, Greenlaw Colliery, their sincere thanks for and high appreciation of the distinguished service rendered by you on the occasion of the disastrous fire at Mauricewood Pit, Penicuik, by which sixty-three workmen lost their lives.

The self-devotion and intrepidity displayed by you and your brave associates in the perilous work of endeavouring to service the entombed men compel the highest admiration. The Directors will ever hold your praiseworthy conduct in grateful remembrance. By order of the Board. Signed: Robert Bell, Chairman. A. W. Turnbull, Secretary.

1

Martha: Christmas and
New Year 1889–1890

The Devil was dancing a jig on the banks of the Leithen. His horns pushed through tufts of matted dry hair and glinted in the sunshine. His cloven hooves left their imprint on the sandy gravel of the river bank and on the fresh grass. His pointed tail switched and flicked through the air with a metallic hiss; it slashed through thistle and dock and ragwort, throwing up sheep dirt and stones and splashes of river water. The Leithen sparkled and sang as it ran down towards the Tweed and the Devil was deliriously happy.

Two figures came scurrying up from the direction of the town, one in a dark dress, one in a white dress. The one in the white dress carried a long stick, the one in the dark dress something shorter. As they came nearer, Martha recognised her granny in the dark dress. She was carrying a poker. The other figure was a monk. He carried a shepherd's crook. It was St Ronan, the patron saint of Innerleithen, and he was damned if he was letting the Devil get away from him this time. Martha's granny brandished her poker and squealed, I'll help you, I'll help you – don't you worry, St Ronan, between us we'll vanquish that heathen devil. St Ronan's habit was white, and Martha saw that his feet beneath it were snowy white and that they stayed that way no matter how much mud or sheep dirt he walked through. When the Devil saw St Ronan and Martha's granny and heard what they had to say his laughter made all the trees up Lee Pen and along the waterside shake. He hopped from one foot to the other on the opposite side of the stream. He shook his tail at them and aimed a deadly kick at St Ronan's head. But St Ronan caught the tail with the crook of his stick and twisted it hard. Martha's granny bashed it with her poker as the Devil howled in pain and landed in the middle of the Leithen. I've got you now,

shouted St Ronan placing a foot on the Devil's neck.
You can drown in God's sweet water. But the Devil just
snorted, opened his mouth and drank all the water.
Then he shook off St Ronan's foot and climbed out
onto the banking. Granny looked surprised. Oh, she
said, it's you. Who else were you expecting said Big
Alex as he pulled straight his waistcoat and adjusted
his collar and tie? He shook hands with St Ronan and
wished him well then looked at his pocket watch on
the end of its long chain and said we'll have to hurry
up or we'll miss the train.

Inside the tunnel Martha could see a crowd of miners in the distance. Most of them faced the walls; they were very busy. They pulled at the walls with their bare hands; none of them had hammers or pickaxes or shovels or any kind of tool. Some of them had their jackets off they sweated so much. As she got nearer, Martha could see they were eating whatever it was that they pulled off the walls. They munched and chewed with great gusto; they pulled at their next mouthful even before they had swallowed. A few crammed their mouths so full and so fast that they gagged; they had a crazed look in their eyes. They were eating puffballs that sprouted white and luminous out of the wet black walls of the tunnel as quick as the miners could pick them. They ate them like apples. Then the puffballs turned into marshmallows. We're having our pudding now one of the miners shouted as the walls turned white and soft, turned into marshmallow that the miners ate through till they reached the sunshine.

Davie Anderson was down the pit and Martha was at the school. Martha and her big sister, Helen, had been sent to live with their granny and grandfather when their mother died not long after Martha was born but their granny was a bad woman. Not that many people knew that because she went to the Kirk twice on a Sunday and wasn't keen on the drink. There was no love in her. She never cuddled Martha and Helen like Phamie's mother did. So Martha and Helen made a secret plan to get rid of her so that they could get to go and live with their Dad and Jess in Shottstown where all the miners lived. They wouldn't get rid of their grandfather; he could go and live with their Auntie Nellie and her man because they'd plenty room and they were cheery folk.

Martha and Helen stole a paper poke out of the kitchen cupboard and went down to the Toll Wood. They filled it up with foxgloves and toadstools and deadly nightshade then took it back to the house. Martha hid the poke under her pinafore until they were able to stuff it into a drawer in their bedroom. Late at night, when their granny and grandfather were sleeping, Martha and Helen sneaked out into their grandfather's shed and boiled the whole lot up on his paraffin stove till there was just a thick puddle left that they scooped into a tin then scooped it from there into their granny's bottle of tonic. One mouthful the next morning was all it took and that was the end of her. By teatime, Martha and Helen were in Shottstown and Jess had them sitting down to plates of cock-a-leekie soup and mince and doughballs. Their Dad was so pleased to see them when he came home that he went straight back out and bought two big bars of Fry's chocolate cream.

We were often as not at school on Christmas Day. New Year's Day was a holiday, but not Christmas. We were at the school that year my Dad was lost because I remember saying a special prayer for him at the service we had in the morning. Then Miss Lillie read us a story. It was *The Little Match Girl.* I've never forgotten it: the girl sent out to sell matches in the depths of winter with just her slippers on and no coat, and no-one would buy any matches from her. The wee soul scared to go home because of the row she'd get (I knew all about that) and lighting all her matches to keep herself warm. The only thing about her that I envied was that her granny was kind. It maybe wasn't the best story to tell us. I wasn't the only one in tears at the end when they find her all frozen in the morning. I couldn't get her out of my head although I cheered up on the way home because we went into Phamie's. Phamie said me and Helen had to come in before we went home because her mother had a surprise for us. We got a surprise from her every year. She knew we'd get nothing at home so she always diddled us up a little parcel, just a little thing; no one had the money for anything fancy. That year she'd made us each a handkerchief with our initials embroidered on the corner and little flowers round about. I knew that I was safe to show it to my grandfather because it was from Phamie's mother and my granny wouldn't dare chuck it on the fire. I could be a bit of a besom though and so away I went home, so pleased with myself, making a big show of it, letting my grandfather see my new favourite handkerchief. You'll be keeping that for the church on Sundays, I suppose, he said. And I said no, I'm going to keep it with my other special things in my white box. This was a wooden box painted white. It had a rose stencilled on the front. I kept it under the bed and it had things in it like a small metal mirror in the shape of an apple that my auntie had given me when she was clearing out a drawer. The mirror had apple leaves for a handle with a silk tassel tied round the stalk. It was inside a leather case marked like apple bark. It had Eve and the Apple stamped in gold writing on the front although you'd have struggled to make it out because it was almost worn off. It was meant for a woman to carry in a bag. I loved to pull it out of its case and peer at myself in the smooth, shiny metal. And there was a miniature pair of scissors that my grandfather had found down the side of an old chair that he'd done up. He reckoned they'd come out of a manicure set. They had the loveliest blue and white handles and a dainty little clip to hold the blades together. There was one of Jaikie's feathers, a fluffy one from when he was young. There was a stone with pretty green markings from out the Leithen, lengths of ribbon, a sprig of white heather for luck, and four-leaved clovers – we were always on the lookout for them. I'd have two or three in the box till they dried out so much they fell to pieces. We had them pressed inside our Bibles too, and I had a piece of yarrow in mine from up Lee Pen. That was one of the things we did in the summer. Jess would bring us blotting paper from the mill where she worked, bits that were no good, that were going to waste, and we'd pick roses and other flowers that we liked and put them in between sheets of blotting paper, put other paper on top, then weigh it down. We had a brick that we'd cleaned up especially for the job. We once tried it with a hollyhock. Phamie's Dad, Big Alex had given us it. He liked his garden. It was thanks to him that the station platform at Innerleithen was always pretty. They had big planters either side of the track. Alex was so proud of them; he always made sure they were colourful and well kept. He grew vegetables too but you got the feeling that that was because he had to, to feed his family. But his face lit up when he was with his flowers: chrysanths, gladioli, dahlias, and fuchsias. He loved them. He bred them, tried for different strains. He had a small glass-house, not many people had them then, but Alex did. So this year he'd tried hollyhocks and he gave one to me and Helen. Now, he says, you'll need to plant it out in the garden. See if your grandfather'll let you plant it beside his shed because it'll need something to lean on, and it'll grow big, maybe even as big as me. Our jaws dropped at the thought of such a huge plant. I don't know what colour it'll be. It could be white or red or any shade of pink in between. And you'll need to remember to water it, at least until it gets going. That must have been a couple of years before my Dad died because I was about five years old when we had the hollyhock. Helen carried it round to my granny's house because she was the biggest and I ran into the shed shouting to my grandfather to get a spade, quick, because we had a flower to plant. He was mending a shoe but gave up after two minutes of us dancing round him. We told him Big Alex had said we should plant it at the side of his shed so that it would get the sun and how big it would be, and he said that if it was that big he'd not be able to see out the window. But give him his due, out he came. Helen already had the trowel and watering can laid out. I lugged the big fork, it would be about twice the size of me, and between us we planted this bloody hollyhock. My grandfather put a whole lot of dung in beside it because nothing was ever planted there and the soil was poor while Helen and I took it in turns to fill the watering can and give it a good soak. And we tended it faithfully. We couldn't let it die. Then we had some good weather, so it grew and grew until it burst out into the loveliest deep red flowers, big and silky, as big as a saucer. Big Alex had to come round to see them we were so pleased with ourselves. They'd win a prize in a show he said as we near burst with pride. All our granny could say was that if we put as much work into what we should be doing about the house it would be a fine day. Everyone ignored her and Big Alex winked at us because he had his back to her and said you could win a medal with them they're so pretty. She just tut tutted and shook her head while Big Alex stood beside the hollyhock to let us see that it was nearly as big as he was just like he'd said it would be.

Helen had been desperate to dry the flowers so we did our usual with a whole stalk of them but it didn't work, they went mouldy. We should have laid them out in the air to dry but we didn't know that then. When we lifted off the brick and the paper all that was there where some mouldy black blotches and the stem all slimy. There was no way we'd be keeping them, no way I could put one into my white box. But the handkerchief from Phamie's mother went in there and I wrapped a piece of dried lavender in it so that every time I opened the box I'd breathe in the scent of it and lay it back down as if it was the Crown Jewels.

Helen had the best thing either of us had in her keepsake box because she had our mother's wedding ring. My Dad kept it for her when our mother died but only gave it to her when she was old enough to look after it herself. I was to get his when his time came. That's what he always told me. That would be to make me feel that I wasn't missing out. I don't suppose he ever thought that his time would come so soon. I never got it though. I wouldn't have wanted it with what happened. But Helen, she was always going to wear our mother's ring when she got married, and she did. It fitted her fine. She was built like our mother, at least that's what people said, people who'd known her. And Helen had a vague memory of her although she was only two when she died, a memory of something pale blue and a voice, singing. When I was small she would make up stories about our mother to satisfy me because, often as we were going to sleep, I'd pester her to tell me about her, what she'd have been doing if she hadn't died, what our life might have been like. And in Helen's stories she was always kind, always motherly, always making delicious cakes or buying us all the best clothes. The poor soul could never have lived up to it. And she was always singing, so Helen would sing her heart out like a wee lintie and I would fall asleep with her voice wavering in my ears and her arm around me, and I just loved her. That was when I was small. When I was older I'd make up my own stories when I was falling asleep, about my mother, about my Dad and Jess and how it would be if we lived with them, and quite often the stories would be about how I would do away with my granny! I was good at thinking up ways of doing that. I was good at justifying it too. As far as I was concerned, God would be able to see through all her God-fearing ways, any God worth his salt at any rate. We weren't even allowed up to the table to eat our food. And it wasn't just that we were children because we had a cousin came to stay with us for a while, Grace her name was, stayed with us when her mother had to go into the hospital, and she was fed at the table. She got the best of stuff while we had to sit on the bench at the fireside supping our tatties and gravy on our knees. I suppose there were plenty worse off than me and Helen. And we always felt it worse at times like Christmas or the New Year when people gathered for parties and the like. Although that year my Dad died was like no other. We all ended up round at Phamie's on New Year's Day which was unheard of. I think that Phamie's mother and Big Alex had decided that we all needed cheering up so they insisted that my granny and grandfather came along to the house and brought us with them. Big Alex assured my granny that there wouldn't be much drinking because all the children would be there and anyway, anyone who would be wanting any would have had enough the night before. There was a pot of stovies on the go and they'd see us in half an hour. That's really good of you, Alex, said my grandfather. We'll be there. And so we were. We all had a quick wash, put on our Sunday best and went round to Phamie's house. Well, I'd never seen the like. You could hardly move for people, and the noise, it was great; people laughing and shouting at one another, children running up and down the stairs and in and out the door. Big Alex got my granny and grandfather sat down near the fire while we disappeared with Phamie and the rest of the gang. I was in my element; any time spent near Phamie's big brother, Tom, was the best time as far as I was concerned. I was daft on him. He was a joker, full of fun. I think I liked him so much because he reminded me of my Dad, that and his curly blonde hair, many's the girl envied him his hair. Tammy Troot his Dad called him, or Doubting Thomas, like in the Bible, or True Thomas. I didn't know who True Thomas was; I just thought it was some kind of opposite to Doubting Thomas. I asked Big Alex one time who True Thomas was and he said that he'd lived a long, long time ago and that he went away with the fairies – not away in the head – away to stay with them. The Queen of the Fairies took a shine to him so she took him away for seven years and when he came back he couldn't tell a lie. I must've looked worried. Big Alex said I did. It would be the thought of not even being able to tell a white lie because I was good at telling them; they could make the difference between getting a skelp or not.

Tom was killed in the war, at Passchendaele. He'd married Jeannie Thomson and they had a son. Her father was the factor at Traquair. She was in Helen's class at the school. We'd walk across to play with her in the holidays. And if the Laird was away we'd get a look round the house, well some bits of it anyway. Jeannie's mother was friends with the housekeeper and we'd get a grand tour. We got to see all the fancy furniture, the bed where Mary Queen of Scots had slept and the beautiful things she'd sewn that hung on the walls. She must have been very handy with a needle because we did embroidery and that gave us an idea how good a seamstress she must have been. I guess she'd learned that in France. We'd heard all about her at the school, about how she was imprisoned on the island in Loch Leven, how she was smuggled out and escaped in a rowing boat, how she nearly died when she fell off her horse near the Hermitage further down the Borders, about the bloodstain that you could still see on the floor at

Holyroodhouse where Rizzio was murdered, and about her getting her head chopped off down in England by Queen Elizabeth. Helen used to embarrass me by telling everyone how, when I first heard the story, I thought it was Queen Elizabeth herself that had done the chopping. And that was the thing that I liked best at Traquair House, Mary Queen of Scots' death mask. I've always had a ghoulish streak. When I first saw it and found out what it was, I got such a fright. But I kept going back for another look until I could stare at it and not want to run away because it looked like you'd imagine a ghost would look: white and smooth. The thought that the wax had been put on Mary's face when she was scarce dead sent a shiver through me, and the thought that that was what she looked like for real kept me staring at it. And she was a Catholic. That was another reason to like her because the very mention of her name would have my granny on her high horse going on about Papes and thanking God we'd had John Knox to keep us all on the straight and narrow. So the thrill we got from going into the little chapel at Traquair was more than doubled when Jeannie's mother would say mind, don't tell your granny you were in here, I'd get the most terrible row. And even better than the Chapel was the priest's hidey hole from the days when being a Catholic was against the law. You opened what looked like a cupboard in one of the upstairs rooms and out of the back of it was a secret staircase. I put my head in but I didn't go down the steps. They were very narrow and I was scared of what I might meet. Then the housekeeper would show us the priest's robes and fold them up to let us see how they could be made to look like cushion covers so that no one would need to know what they were.

It was bonny at Traquair. The house was like a castle but small enough to feel friendly. Flowers grew about the walls and gave it a homely feel. And we always got the story of the Bear Gates. Standing at the door of the house you look all the way up a big grassy drive with trees either side and see them in the distance, big gates with a stone bear on top of each gate post. If you take a walk round by Traquair village and look at them close up, they're grey with lichen. They're always shut. The story goes that in 1745, after Bonny Prince Charlie rode out and away, the Earl locked them behind him and threw away the keys saying they'd never be opened again till a Stuart was on the throne. My Dad always used to say it's either that or he just lost the keys. They're shut to this day, anyway. Not that I was ever that interested in the goings-on of Earls or Princes, they never seemed to make much odds to those who had to work for a living.

Phamie's youngest brother was sitting on Martha's knee. She sang Wee Willie Winkie even though it wasn't bedtime and baa baa black sheep and hey diddle diddle and Humpty Dumpty. She took his hand and circled his palm three times saying round and round the garden went the teddy bear. Then she did one step, two steps and tickled him right there under the oxter. He squirmed and wriggled with delight so to get him to stay still, Martha sang sing a song of sixpence, a pocket full of rye, four and twenty blackbirds baked in a pie and there on the table was the biggest pie Martha had ever seen. Phamie's mother stood, dish towel in hand, admiring it. Steam curled out of a hole in the top. When the pie was opened, there were only seventeen birds and they were jackdaws, not blackbirds and they began to squawk as they flew out of the pie dish and out through the open door. But the heat of the oven had dried them up, desiccated them, so that they crumbled and the remains of the jackdaws became a fall of sooty spores on the snow-covered ground. And the snow had turned into thick wet blotting paper which absorbed and smudged the sooty crumbs till they looked like the imprints of so many mouldering flowers.

But that New Year's Day day at Phamie's we all had great fun. And the highlight, for me and Helen anyway, was when we discovered that her cat had kittens. We were chasing one another when Tom ran outside and into the shed. He stopped dead in his tracks and we all stotted into one another at the back of him. He turned round, shushed us all and said look, Queenie's had kittens. And right enough, there she lay on an empty sack in the far corner with what looked like five small hairless creatures suckled into her. You'd better fetch mother said Tom, she'll know what to do for the best. So Phamie's mother whirled out of the house, all cheery and flushed, bits of hair twirling round her face, wiping her hands on her pinny and giving me and Helen a big smile and a hello before she chased us all away from the shed door to see what was going on. Well, Queenie, she said, what have you brought me? The cat meowed at her. You're all right, I'll not touch them. She moved aside to let us all see. You'll need to shush, Queenie needs peace and quiet. But Helen piped up will they not freeze to death out here? And Phamie's mother said no, because she'd bring them all into the house once everyone went away. And she shooed us all back in where it was noisy and warm and poured us glasses of ginger wine. We called it wine but there was no alcohol in it. You got a little bottle of concentrated ginger at the chemist's and made it up with sugar and water. I loved anything with ginger in it, still do. So we all trooped into the living room and Phamie announced that Queenie'd had kittens and that we'd seen them and that her mother was fetching them in later on. Bill Johnson said that'll be for your Dad to drown them, then, eh? The looks on our faces must have been a picture for Big Alex said not these ones, Bill, I promised them that the cat could keep her first litter. I can still see my granny's sour face in the corner. Far better rid of them, Alex. And I'm warning you, I'll chuck stones at them if they come round to do their business in my garden.

I was relieved when a man who'd come up from near Dumfries to work beside Alex at the station began to play the penny whistle. Peggy Meikle joined in with the melodeon, and, as the afternoon wore on, Big Alex and two or three others got the spoons out and made a great racket. Jimmy Duthie had a go at the paper and comb but he'd had too much drink and kept slavering into the paper so that it got too wet to play. Then they had a breather and we got stuck into the stovies that Phamie's mother had made. I had mine out of a cup because there were no bowls or plates left, and they were just how I like them, made with nothing more than beef dripping, onion, potato and a good dose of salt and pepper. Then we got some cake. Phamie's mother had made a Madeira cake, someone had brought a sultana loaf, and there was shortbread; I was in my element. It was all over too soon and before we knew it, we were being told it was time to go home and my granny was at the door wrapping a scarf around my grandfather's neck and him annoyed at her because we were only two doors away.

Helen was so excited about the kittens she could hardly get to sleep. I knew without her saying that she wanted one and that would be a no from my granny. Then in between being excited she'd get herself in a state about how anyone could drown kittens, and was I sure they didn't feel anything when they went into the water? I had to be quick and say no, the shock of the cold water knocked them out right away. Then she panicked in case Phamie's mother forgot to take them into the house and they'd all be frozen by the morning. So I had to get up and look out of the window to see if the lights were still on along the road and if the shed door was shut. Then there was a roar from the living room to settle down and get to sleep – what did we think we were playing at and we'd better not have opened that window? My granny couldn't sleep at night if she thought there was a window open. Next thing, we could see her shadow in the light of the scarce-open door.

So I scrambled back into my bed and for a while it was as if nothing could take away the lift we'd got from our afternoon round at Phamie's till Helen said I wonder if the cold water knocked our Dad out right away? As it turned out I don't think it was the water that killed him. I think he must've just run out of air. Those who found him said that a lot of them were sitting up against the walls as if they'd known what was coming and had just waited quietly. They reckon it's just like going to sleep, that there wouldn't have been a struggle, and I hope so, I bloody hope so. Of course we didn't know that at the New Year, we didn't find out these things till the Spring; it was the end of March before they got them out. They'd had the first Inquiry by then, the week before the New Year. They seemed to think that a door hadn't been working properly and that it had let smoke into places it shouldn't have been. But the word was that the Company had got off lightly. It took a while for all that to get down to us in Innerleithen.

At heart we knew that we'd never see our Dad again, that there was no way he could have survived that long although when you're a child, or maybe even when you're grown-up, there's always a bit of you that's looking for a miracle. I would still tell myself stories about how he'd survived but they were more and more far-fetched; by now the rescuers were angels or fairies.

Shadrach, Meshach and Abednego were being prepared for the fiery furnace. The soldiers had stoked the fires to seven times hotter than was enough to kill a man and now they bound the three who had dared to not pray to the King. They bound each in turn, each one in a wide strip of white linen. Shadrach turned around and Martha gasped – he had the face of the man who had won the quoits competition at last year's Games. His eyes were closed and he looked as if he was concentrating very hard. They moved on to Meshach and, as he was rotated, Martha realised that he was Johnny, her Dad's pal. He winked at Martha and said your Dad's next. Martha said but I thought it was Abednego and Johnny said not this time, him and his friends are being furnaced next week. Then the binders turned the third figure towards her and it was her Dad. He laughed when he saw her. Why the long face? God wouldn't let me burn. I'm scared he will. Do you think he'd let me burn when your granny's done all that praying? I don't trust him. I think he might be a liar. Don't you worry; the three of us'll be out of there in as long as it takes to make a slice of toast. And at that, the soldiers flung them on a cart and headed for the mouth of the furnace. As they tipped in their load, the soldiers turned to ash the heat was so great.

After a while a tall man in a frock coat and top hat came along and looked in. I can see four men walking about in there. Pull them out; this should not be. And out came Doddie Livingstone and Johnny Glass and Davie Anderson and Big Alex. Big Alex was in his shirt sleeves and collarless. He was red in the face and wiped the sweat from his brow. Well, he said, it's a good job I was on the early shift today.

Davie Anderson was down the pit and Martha was at the school. Martha was living in Innerleithen with her granny and grandfather because her mother was dead and her Dad didn't like to take her and her big sister, Helen, away because they'd been there since they were anything and it would have broken their grandfather's heart. Their grandfather was a quiet soul but too soft when it came to dealing with their granny. She had Martha and Helen working their fingers to the bone and she was mean when it came to dishing out the food. She had a fiery temper and wouldn't think twice about giving either of them a skelp. And she was always going on about not having enough money, so one day she came home with a big bag of matches that Martha and Helen were to go out and sell. She sent them on the train up to Peebles because more people lived there. She sent them in their stocking soles with no coats on so that people would feel sorry for them. It was Old Year's Night and the snow had fallen heavy the day before. Martha and Helen trudged up and down the High Street in Peebles but nobody would buy their matches. The loveliest smells came out of the hotels but Martha and Helen had not a penny between them to buy anything to eat. They were supposed to get the last train but when it came four o'clock and they hadn't sold any matches, Helen said I know, we'll catch an earlier train and go up to Leithen Lodge before we go home. The people there have got plenty of money; they'll buy the matches from us. They were scared to go home with none sold.

So they jumped on the 4 o'clock train but they had to sneak out of the station at Innerleithen in case Big Alex saw them and took them home. Then they tramped all the way up the Leithen Road even though their feet were so blue with the cold that they couldn't feel them. When they got to Leithen Lodge they rapped the door but there was a party going on inside. The people made too much noise to be able to hear them and nobody came. Martha and Helen both felt like crying. Helen said we'll wait a while and try again. Come on, we'll coorie in here, in this corner where there's some shelter from the roof until the noise dies down. Martha and Helen got colder and colder. Martha said could we not light a match to warm ourselves up, and Helen said no, we need to keep them all to get as much money as we can when we sell them. But they were shivering so much that Helen said well maybe just one, and she took one out and rubbed it against the wall. It sputtered and burned warm and bright like a candle and to Martha and Helen it felt like a big stove. Then it burnt out. Helen couldn't get another one out quick enough. This time the light made the wall see-through and there was the big table all set for the party. There was a big goose right in the middle all golden and shiny. There were pheasants happed up in bacon, two ham joints and heaps of roasted potatoes and carrots and peas with lumps of butter all melting down into them. Martha and Helen gasped when the goose jumped down off the table and came dancing across to them, a huge knife and fork stuck in its breast, three pheasants on either side skittering across the floor to keep up with it. But the lights went out and all they were left with was the cold, thick wall. Helen lit another match and the next thing they knew, they were under a Christmas tree. It was covered in candles and hanging from the branches were lovely pictures just like the ones Helen liked to look at in the calendars in Smail's window. They reached their hands out to touch them just as the match went out but the lights of the candles shot up into the sky and turned into stars. One fell back down again and Martha and Helen knew that meant someone had died. I wonder if a star fell when our mother died, said Martha, and Helen said I wish she hadn't. Just think what it would have been like if we'd had our mother to look after us. And she lit another match. The wall went all bright and Martha and Helen could see their mother in the glow. She had on a blue blouse and there was a shininess all round her. She had the kindest, warmest smile that Martha had ever seen. *Martha and Helen shouted at her to stay, not to disappear like the goose or the Christmas tree when the match went out. Then they bundled all the matches together and lit the lot. They burned brighter than daylight and their mother took Martha and Helen into her arms and flew up to Heaven.*

In the morning, the people in Leithen Lodge found Martha and Helen frozen to death leaning against the front wall. There was a bundle of burnt out matches in Helen's hand. They must have been trying to keep warm, they said. Whose children are they anyway? And when they found out that their granny had sent them out in all that snow to sell matches with not so much as a coat on their backs or a pair of shoes on their feet, they put her in the jail and threw away the key.

Davie Anderson was down the pit and Martha was at the school. Martha and her big sister, Helen, lived in Penicuik with him and Jess, in Shottstown where all the miners lived. Jess had made a pretty bedroom for them: they had a bed each with patchwork quilts on them and white sheets with embroidered edges. She'd given up work to look after them and was always cooking and cleaning and mending and washing and sewing and going her messages. She was a good cook. Every dinner and teatime Martha and Helen came in and sat down at the table to home-made soup, meat and tatties, and rice pudding or apple dumpling or jam sponge – all their favourite things.

Jess: 1889–1890

And when we found out what had happened – that more than a few of them had lived for God knows how long – it's no wonder that I went a bit crazy. The thought of them sitting there waiting to die, knowing that that was all there was in front of them, was too much to bear. All I could think about for a while after we found that out was how I was going to kill Love and maybe some of the rest of them too, but him to start with. I got myself so worked up one night that I grabbed Davie's big knife and set off to murder him. My plan was to catch him on his way home from work but for a good job it came on bucketing rain and I got so wet that it cooled my ardour. What a state I was in. I held the knife against the skin of my own wrist before I burst into tears and ran away. I never told anyone but Sadie.

But that wasn't until after, after they'd found them and they'd all been buried. We were well into the Spring by then. What a long six months that was. There was always something to hold things up. Sadie and the other women went back to the Company offices, and not just once. They bawled and shouted at Love, pleaded with him to give them their men and their boys back. But he could never give them the answer they wanted: the fire was still burning; there was fire damp so no-one could get down to see how things were; the fire had broken out again; then it was flooded; expert advice was needed. The women threatened to come back every day until the pit was cleared but it was November before a start was made to pump the water out. And it was filthy, full of rusty-coloured sediment. The burn they emptied it into looked like a streak of dirty blood. It stained the river all the way down to the sea at Musselburgh. There were those who complained but how else were they supposed to get rid of it. And there must have been a hell of a lot because it took until March to empty the pit.

After the recovery of the first 27 bodies, further exploration was stopped by flooding consequent upon the destruction of the pumping engines and gear at the 160 fathom level. Water had risen to the floor of the 120 fathom level when they commenced clearing the mine on 5th November, 1889.

A Worthington pump with two 14-inch steel cylinders and two 7-inch double-acting rams was run down on a bogey carriage on the east rail of the main incline to the surface of the water, and then gradually lowered to the bottom of the incline as the water was got under.

Water pumped out of Mauricewood and Greenlaw, its sister pit, emptied into the River North Esk at a day level on the riverbank near Auchendinny station. The Valleyfield, Esk, and Dalmore paper mills all emptied their waste into this same river: mothers warned their children not to play in it.

5 5

We just had to keep busy. For those who had children that was less of a struggle; they had more than enough on their plates. But for me on my own... well... it was as if my life was crumbling; there were times when I felt that I wanted to die. I couldn't bear to be idle or to be in an empty house. I'd go out nearly every night or have someone round to keep me company. I'd go to Sadie's or my mother's or my sister's, or I'd have friends from my work round and we'd knit and have a blether. Then there was the Church Fellowship; they would have a social every now and then. Or there would be a concert to go to. I'll never forget the night we went to see the Salvation Army's re-enactment of *The Parable of the Ten Virgins*. The town had been speaking about it for weeks. It was in November when the dark nights were well and truly in and it was hard not to despair about them ever getting anyone else out of the pit. The grief of it all was still so fresh that I'd be alright one minute then dissolved in tears the next and nothing I could do about it. I persuaded Sadie to go with me to get us out of the house. I felt there was bound to be a spectacle of some kind that would take our minds off things because people weren't very keen on the Salvationists when they'd first started about the year before. There had been a riot in their new hall in the summer; one man had ended up in the jail for a week. So we went. But the only spectacle was the rammy caused by some of the crowd. They were out to make trouble and it was all too chaste for their liking. But if I'd nothing lined up, I'd clean the house from top to bottom or I'd bake even if it was a Sunday. I couldn't sit still. And there were nights I hardly slept. How could I? The thought of Davie lying somewhere and no decent burial.

Sundays were the worst. For a good job I went to the Church. I've seen me go twice in the one day just for something to do although I loved the singing and it was a comfort to be there, people round about and the Minister such a decent man. It made me feel there would be some consolation at the end for us all. Although that feeling was pretty short-lived when I went back to an empty house and an empty bed. And as time went by I couldn't see how anyone's God would let Mauricewood happen. When the Minister visited, I'd ask him questions, but I knew what the answers would be before he came out with them and none of them relieved the pain. I couldn't get over the feeling that I was being spoken to like a child. I still went to the Kirk but when the prayers were announced I stopped bowing my head and I kept my eyes open.

Then in the December there was the Inquiry, the first one. Mr Gladstone himself had said to make sure that there was one. And the unions, they were just getting going then; Keir Hardie spoke up for us. So they knew that plenty were watching what came out of it but, like I said, it made no difference. Might as well have not bothered. The word came out right at the end of the month so there wasn't much good cheer that New Year, not that there could have been with however many of them still lying in that hole.

A Government Inquiry under the Coal Mines Regulation Act, 1887, into the fatal accident at Mauricewood Colliery was held at the High Court in Edinburgh on 26th December 1889 and for three working days thereafter, led by Henry Johnson, advocate, and Thomas Bell, one of Her Majesty's Inspectors of Mines.

The commissioners had had no access to the mine workings. H.M.I. Atkinson had made a brief visit to the Mauricewood offices, looked at plans, and taken witness statements from the Company and its employees, but the initial Report was issued with the missing dead unrecovered and the mine still flooded.

Workers did not trust the Inspector. Would he not have a vested interest in maintaining the reputed thoroughness of his previous inspections? The men had hung around the pit trying to keep an eye on what was happening but the police moved them off on the orders of the manager.

2 15

Section 16 of the Coalmines Regulation Act 1887 stated that, 'there must be at least two shafts or outlets through which every seam being worked shall have communication, so that such shafts or outlets shall afford separate means of ingress and egress available to persons employed in every such seam'.

The miners claimed that there was no second means of ingress and egress available at the 160 fathom level. The Commission thought differently. It maintained that the road connecting Mauricewood to Greenlaw at the 80 fathom level was sufficient to meet the terms of the act, and exonerated the Company.

The previous manager, Mr Kirkwood, had begun cutting a second outlet in the spirit of the 1887 Act, but Mr Love, the new manager, stopped this as it was expensive. The Commission of Inquiry accepted and sympathised with the cost considerations involved, and no blame was accorded to the Company.

156

The upset or upcast was a narrow shaft lined with wood and was tinder dry. It contained a pipe carrying water out of the mine and steam pipes connected to the underground pumps. These pumps worked for eighteen hours a day. A ladder ran the full length of the upset.

To climb its full length required strength and stamina. In nearly half a mile of vertical climbing, the heat from the steam pipes would make a man sweat so much that by the time he reached the top, it would be as if he had waded across a jungle river.

The upcast was designated the alternative escape route. But this narrow space and the heat generated within it could not have been regarded as the second exit required by section 16 of the Coalmines Regulation Act, 1887. And in any case, the fire had started near the bottom of it.

William Hunter, a former Mauricewood worker, stated in a public letter that, three years previously, he and forty others were trapped below for many hours when trucks derailed and rendered the incline impassable. They waited at the bottom until the track was repaired rather than use the upcast to escape.

6 15

The Inquiry heard evidence from thirty witnesses – ten called on behalf of the Shotts Iron Company, eighteen for the Miners' Federations and two who had independently volunteered information. Their report was written on 21st February 1890 and issued in the form of a Parliamentary Blue Book on March 17th 1890.

At the date when evidence was led to the Fatal Accident Inquiry on 26th December, 1889, the water stood about 23 fathoms below the 120 fathom level. The mine was reported clear of water on 18th March, 1890, when the work of recovering those still missing was at once commenced.

The only independent expert opinion sought by the Commission concerned the arrangement whereby the upcast passed through the 80 fathom enginehouse. The poor quality of the enginehouse door, and modifications made to it, allowed smoke to short-circuit into the incline, and, from there, into the whole of the lower workings.

The door was not designed to self-close and thereby maintain correct air flow. Also, an air vent that drew in good air had been built into it because the enginehouse became so hot that it was suffocating for the men who worked there. Commissioners recommended improvement to ensure proper closure.

5

Above ground, a 5.5m diameter Waddle fan running at 45rpm assisted by heat from the steam pipes provided an airflow at the pit bottom estimated at 7m³/s. Leakage and the practice of bleeding small quantities to ventilate engine-houses resulted in flows to east and west sides of almost exactly 1m³/s.

A Waddle fan looked like a very big, very narrow waterwheel whose angled blades captured air. It was made of wood and worked on the principle of centrifugal force. However, at Mauricewood, it did not develop very high pressures and the network permitted perhaps nine tenths waste leakage of air.

The mines inspector seemed dissatisfied with his findings in relation to the eighty fathom engine-room door being the fatal cause of the recirculation of fire products. But at the time of his initial report, inspection of the lower parts of the mine was impossible due to fire and rising water.

In 1984, A. Gracie and B. Job, mining engineers, suggested that air flow must have been reversed much further in than the eighty fathom engine-room door. This would explain the fatal density of the smoke and why fresher air circulated in the East workings where men survived 'for some time'.

11 15

The Report stressed that the cause of the fire was not its main concern. It did not publish any witness testimony. Neither did it draw attention to the management of the mine in terms of prevention of future incidents. It stated simply that the cause of the fire was accidental.

Smoking was commonplace down the pit and the men's head-mounted lamps contained a naked flame. The upcast, where the fire started, was lined with wood rendered tinder-dry from the heat of the steam pipes. Unused timber and rubbish was dumped at its foot. There had been a fire in 1886.

The men carried a variety of naked lights; most used the traditional brass tally lamp, as made by A. C. Glass of Dalkeith, which clipped to cap or clothing, but the Roslin firm of candle-makers, Dicksons, still did a thriving business in the manufacture of candles for the mining industry.

Safety lamps had been available for some time but were not universally popular; their level of illumination was lower: miners claimed that they damaged eyesight, some managers that it resulted in more accidents. Their use tended to be restricted to established 'fiery mines'. Mauricewood was not considered a fiery mine.

2

January's a cruel month: long dark nights; going to work and back in the dark; struggling to get out of bed in the morning; the water pipe outside frozen. I always got myself organised with a full kettle before I went to my bed.

The Minister was good to all of us who were grieving. He'd come round and sit a while of a night-time to see how we were or to see if there was anything that the Church could help with. The Church had a Mission at Fieldsend, right in the heart of Shottstown. Many's a body they saved from the poor house.

He was a clever man, the Minister, came from through about Castle Douglas. He was brought up on a farm so he was no stranger to work, and used to the ways of working folk, not like some of those ministers who'd never lifted a hand.

He kept us well entertained at church socials and days out. And at the Sunday School he'd tell exciting stories about the time he worked in a rough part of Edinburgh, about the bad boys getting into fights, about them throwing things at the Sunday school teachers, how they got the better of the police, and ambushed the do-gooders that were sent to try and help them to be upstanding Christian bodies. He could always laugh at himself, Mr Crockett, and it would have taken a pretty sharp person to get the better of him. He was big, more than six feet three and not skinny. Then he had that big beard and thick hair. And he was strong. The children loved his stories, and not just the children. I always felt that he was secretly on the side of the so-called baddies. He always let you know if they were neglected through drink or had no mothers.

He must have been at odds with himself around the time of Mauricewood though. Not that it showed. He was his usual unfailing self. We knew he wrote articles and stories that sometimes got him into trouble with folk in the Kirk who took things too seriously. And we knew that his family weren't too keen either because they had been Cameronians in the old days, and writing was too much like cavorting with the Devil for their liking. But within a few years of Mauricewood he gave up being our Minister in Penicuik. He became a bit of a sensation; we were all reading his books. I was in Edinburgh by then, working as a housekeeper to Robert, my second husband, and feeling a bit homesick, but when I read Mr Crockett's books it was as if I could hear his deep, warm voice and it was a comfort. I could imagine him striding up and down just as if he was in front of the congregation, holding his lapels and keeping us all entranced with his stories. I liked his stories; I liked that there were plenty strong women in them. I always fancied myself as Winsome Charteris: in charge of my own farm, ordering the men about, driving them all daft with my good looks. I could just see myself in a lilac sun bonnet like Winsome has on when the young Minister first spies her with her skirt hoicked up above her knees in the laundry tub by the side of the burn. And I liked that those with the airs and graces always got taken down a peg or two.

He wasn't the Minister when I got married to Davie. It was Mr Hamilton then. He was much more traditional I suppose you might say. There were a good few in the congregation who were always very keen to remind Mr Crockett about what a good Minister Mr Hamilton had been. Many's the Sunday I've heard him thanking those who had written to him with suggestions for how he might conduct his affairs. I was never quite sure just how far his tongue was stuck in his cheek. I'd have been more than happy if it had been him that had married us. Not a body in Shottstown would have said a word against him; he was welcome in every house there because he was one of those that made sure we didn't starve when all the men were lost.

In the wake of Mauricewood, he entered into Penicuik's sorrows. He and his workers in the mission areas comforted the bereaved, provided winding sheets for the dead and daily necessities for the living. The disaster lay heavily in his memory. Many recollections of it found their way into his work.

In 1894 Crockett was invited to contribute to the Christian Socialist publication, *Vox Clamantium*. He wrote a story describing a mine disaster and castigating greedy mine owners. Still later, in *Vida*, 1907, his memory of Mauricewood becomes part of the plot; the lack of the second exit is again stressed.

He has watched miners coming up from their work at Mauricewood, tired and dirty; he has been in their homes and knows their habits; and he has realised and resented on their behalf the cramped unnatural lives they lead, the exhausting labour that left *those returning from underground fully silent*.

When disaster struck the men were no better than rats caught in a trap set for them by Incubus and Company, and baited with thirty shillings a week. But the senior partner was a pious man, and had often prayed for them – only he had not finished the second exit.

7 12

Three boys bending low to take the awkward corners, leaping aside to avoid some laden wagon, raced through the smother, the downdraught pushing deadly smoke along the working faces as they took one dark archway after another, scrambling over dangerous heaps of rubbish in their zeal to warn their comrades.

So, at the word, the long lines of half-naked men dropped their tools, pick or drill or hammer or gellock, and ran fast for the incline where one, at the sight of the smoke and flames shouted, Hear to me, lads, we had better get to the prayin, yon's death.

The Minister sat in the cage with two boys in his arms. The rough wet brattice cloths that had been placed over them charred almost to a cinder. Dairsie Gordon's face was burnt and blackened.

   He handed the boys out into careful hands.

   'I am going down again, he said.

...they were found after seven months underwater, their bodies almost perfectly preserved by the iron which the water held in solution. Some had fallen forward. Some had simply sunk down, and one of the boys who ran to warn the men was found with his head on the parental knees.

7 12

I'd got to know Davie through Sadie. Johnny Glass had lodged with him and Maggie when he first came to work at Mauricewood. Sadie would tell me stories about him. He'd always have a daft thing to say and often as not you wouldn't see it coming. He'd bother Sadie about Johnny. He'd say *you must get an awfy fright, hen, when you waken up in the morning.* And when she looked puzzled he would point at Johnny and say *wakening up next to that.* He'd torment the life out of people but they'd always lap it up. They'd be more than happy to be called *tattie heid* or *ba'heid.* And he loved to sing. He'd go about singing *Gae bring to me a pint of wine* or *Ae Fond Kiss* and he couldn't see a lettuce but he'd burst into *Come, let us be joyful.* There were times when you could see him far enough because you'd heard it so often but just the look on his face. He'd put on that cheeky smile and be so cheery that you'd be giggling before you knew where you were. Not that he didn't have his moods. He could go in the pet like anybody. And I've seen him carry a grudge for years. He never spoke to Jimmy Smith, the despatcher at Harper's, after he was convinced he'd got him laid off one time.

So when he came to work in the mill, I felt as if I knew him. He'd taken it hard when Maggie died. Never went near a woman for long enough. Although I think there were a good few who would have had him because he was well liked. There was one that was sweet on him, I can't remember her name, brassy blonde, worked in the mill. She'd been a pal of his sister's; her man had run away and left her not that long after they were married. Some said he was running away from debts but most people reckoned he just couldn't handle her. She'd appear on Davie's doorstep with something that she'd cooked or something that she needed fixed. He never dared let her in. She gave up after a while when they got a new grocery assistant at the Store and she took to running after him: just a young lad, but green. She told him that her man was dead and took him to live with her. His mother was none too pleased; she'd been too used to having his wages.

Davie'd got a start with the potchers – that's where they cut up the stuff to make the paper and bleach it before it goes through to the beaters, the men who make up the mix for whatever paper recipe they're making. That was always the joke – that he was potching by day and poaching by night because it was no secret that he was an enthusiastic poacher. He never got caught. Had a good few close calls right enough but I'm sure the gamekeepers weren't too worried by the likes of Davie catching a few trout. They weren't too keen on giving away too many salmon though. I gave away his poaching gear to his younger brother all except the big knife, it was a handy size. He regretted how he got that knife. When he was on the farm, he'd been sent to the blacksmith's to get something fixed and when he got back there it was lying on the floor of the cart. He denied having seen it, let them think it must have been the tramp that was in the smiddy that day. Poor man got chased the next time.

And of course he had his dog. A lot of the miners had dogs. They'd usually keep lurchers because they were good runners and were good for catching rabbits and hares. But Davie never had a lurcher. He got his first dog from the farmer at Macbiehill where he'd grown up. It was a springer spaniel. Then he had Tweed, he was a retriever cross. He appeared home with him one day with a story about how he had been passing the dairy when he'd noticed this bonny young dog running about. Well if you knew Davie you'd know that he would have to speak to it. He had a way with dogs, had a soft spot for them. And when he asked the men who were busy unloading milk churns whose it was, they said his if he wanted it. When they'd been out that morning they'd met a farmer away to shoot it because it was no use to him, and the man collecting the milk had said no, no, you'll no do that, there's plenty as would have a bonny dog like that. And so Davie took him home. It worshipped him that dog, followed him everywhere. When it was time for him to come home, it'd trot along to the end of the street to wait for him and not move until it was whistled on. When Davie never came back the poor thing was lost, kept looking for him, kept looking at me as if to say where is he. I don't know how often I had to go and fetch him from the corner of the street. He'd sit there, looking out along the Edinburgh Road. Old Peggy Hutchison would give him a drink of water and some scraps if it didn't look as if I was coming. He was such a canny dog. The children would get him to play with their ball or, one time, one of the girls had him diddled up with a ribbon around his neck and an old straw bonnet on his head. But there were some bad ones. Once I went looking for him and he wasn't at his usual corner. I could hear yelping and a commotion coming from the field. There was a crowd of boys and I could see they were chucking stones and that two or three of them had sticks. Well, it's a wonder they didn't hear me shouting in Portobello. I took the dog to live with my mother and father after that. But oh, he pined. It was as if he couldn't understand what had happened. He just faded away. It nearly broke my heart. My father buried him at the foot of his garden. He wasn't a man to show much feeling but I'd never seen such a look on his face as when he dug that grave. He rammed the spade into the ground so hard it frightened me.

My father thought a lot of Davie. He was comfortable with him. They could speak about the garden or the fishing and the pair of them liked a flutter. If someone was running a book as like as not they'd know about it – it'd be the horses or the running. They always had a bet on the New Year Sprint at Powderhall. Johnny Maule at the foot of Napier Street ran a book. Davie'd liked gambling a bit too much when he was young. So his sister told me. Until he lost his grandfather's good pocket watch playing brag – not even his to gamble. He was in a terrible sweat, up all night till he won it back.

My mother and father weren't so sure when I told them

who I was going out with but that was before they got to know him. All they could think of at first was that he was a widower with two children, and what was I doing when I could have any number of younger men with no encumbrances. But, well, the first time I brought him home he had them roaring and laughing at stories from when he was young and daft. To her dying day my mother never forgot the story about the old ploughman at Macbiehill who was always looking for the jaggiest cones to scratch his piles. And by the time he'd helped my father mend the roof of his shed and declared that my mother's rice pudding was the best he'd ever tasted, that was it. From that day on they thought the sun shone out of his backside. And that was what I fell for too. He'd taken to falling in with me and Sadie on our way to the mill in the morning and sometimes on the way home. Sadie would tease me, say it was me that was the attraction, and she was right.

We first walked out one Sunday afternoon. I scarcely heard what the sermon was that day. I'd never really been out with anybody else. There was a bit of me still hankered after Martin Stark. But away we went, down the waterside and round by Glencorse Kirk. It's bonny around there, bonny woods and a burn running through it. That was where Mr Crockett said a prayer for Robert Louis Stevenson. Word had come from Samoa asking him if he would. The Minister at Glencorse was his teacher and it meant a lot to him. Mr Crockett spoke highly of Robert Louis Stevenson. They wrote to each other for years. He was ever grateful for the suggestion that he write in his own tongue because that was what had lit the fire under his book writing. But Davie and me knew nothing about that then. All we knew was that we liked one another's company and the more we got to know one another the more that liking grew and that it was round by Glencorse Kirk that he first took hold of my hand to help me over a dyke and that my hand stayed where it was and sent a tingle all through me until he gave me a kiss just before we came out of the wood. And that was that.

We got married in my mother's house. Mr Hamilton came at a Saturday dinner time and we went off for the afternoon to Edinburgh. We wandered up and down the High Street looking into the closes. We spat on the Heart of Midlothian in front of St Giles then looked in all the shop windows in Princes Street. There was a grocer's there that had our jaws dropping at things we never saw in Penicuik, things we'd never even heard of. And Princes Street Gardens were beautiful. We sat on the grass there and were never happier eating sweeties that we'd treated ourselves to. I can still taste those rose and violet creams, and Davie had some Russian caramels. Then, instead of going up the Scott Monument we birled down to Leith on a tram, up on top, of course. And what a great view we had, right across the water to Fife. That was when they had the horses pulling the trams, not long before they put up the cables. I liked the horse-drawn ones; you felt as if you were in a grand carriage they were so well done out and looked after. Then we got the train home. My mother had sandwiches and a cake waiting for us, and a few neighbours came in and we all had a drink till they walked us down to Davie's house. That was to be my first house as a married woman. For the first time in years I never went to the church on the Sunday morning. I had better things to be doing! But hell, I'm sure I must have blushed to the roots of my hair when the Minister asked where I'd been when we came out the church the next week.

I liked having my own house. We were still in Imrie Place then. We didn't move to Manderston Place until Davie was back in the pit because it was built by the Company for their workers. The houses in Manderston Place were new, with separate sculleries but no gardens. People were always moaning about that, that and the state of the lavvies and the middens. It took a bit of getting used to. My mother and father's house had its own lavvie with us being nearer the edge of town; my father buried the waste once a week in a pit in the garden. But when you'd no garden, well, it all went on the midden. It was a foul mess: cinders, ash, folks' cooking scraps and any rubbish they couldn't burn in the fire went onto the midden – a big stinking heap between the backs of the houses. Just as well it got shifted nearly every day by the council. Then there was Auld Jock Paterson; he emptied the dry toilets of the houses that belonged to Harper's Mill. He would come round with his horse and cart and shovel it up and take it up to spread on his fields. He had a small farm just up the hill that him and his sister looked after. She did the milk and he did the scaffying to give them a bit more money. I don't know how he stood the smell; it must have been all through his clothes. Mind, he was forever whuffing snuff up his nose. And I don't know how much acquainted him and his sister were with Godliness but they certainly weren't with cleanliness. Jim Duffy once told me how his mother sent him up one morning to get a jug of milk and there was a mouse in the ladle Jock's sister lifted out to get the milk. She never turned a hair, just tipped the mouse out and dipped the ladle in. Jim didn't bother with milk on his porridge that morning.

But at least Manderston Place was mine from the start, not so many memories there although we took some furniture Davie had from when Maggie was alive; we couldn't afford not to, and I saved up and got myself a few nice things. My dresser was second-hand but you'd never have known, and my Aunty Mary gave me two willow pattern plates to put on it.

In the first winter we were in, I decided I was going to make a new rag rug but I was going to make it bigger than any we'd had before. So I worked and worked on this damned rug till in the end it was too big. Davie was always tripping on it then he'd swear and I'd get annoyed at him, tell him to lift his feet because I was very pleased with my Sunday rug. The dog liked it; he could get a good stretch. But I never made one as big again. Davie teased me, don't make it too big, he'd say, I don't want to lose my good looks by falling in the fire, or, our name's Anderson not Carnegie, it's not a mansion we live in.

I made all my own curtains and I got the loveliest chintzed cotton one time, paid a pretty penny for it, to make myself a quilted bedspread. Sky blue on one side and peach on the other; it only went on for show! I folded it up every night and laid it on the chair. I liked sewing and I liked cooking and baking and that was just as well because Davie liked his food. It was a pleasure to cook for him because he enjoyed everything I made. Well just about, he was never too struck with grouse; he always said it was too strong. We were well off compared to some because we both worked. Not that we ate like kings but we ate well. Them as had big families did well if the man got scraps of meat off the bone that made the soup. Although you could fairly stretch a bit meat if you knew what you were doing; a load of suet dumplings on the top would soon fill you up. Only thing I didn't like cooking was tripe. To me it smelled more like something you should be making glue with. But my mother would always cook extra and send a bowlful down for him. She boiled it first, that was what caused the stink, then stewed it in milk with plenty of onions. Every now and then I'd try some because I liked the taste of the onions but I could only ever stomach a couple of spoonfuls. I'd end up getting a chewy bit and that would be that. But I loved all the other cheaper things we could get. Liver was one of Davie's favourites. Kidneys, he liked them with ham and egg, and stuffed heart, that always made a tasty change. We were lucky too, having the garden at my father's. It kept us going in potatoes and cabbages, turnips, beetroot, sprouts, and every year Davie would try cauliflower. He gave up trying to grow carrots; he never seemed to be able to get rid of the carrot fly. Every now and then he'd have another go but often as not we'd be lucky to get a plateful. And he'd a few fruit bushes: rasps and blackcurrants and a gooseberry.

I always made rasp jam. He loved it on a piece with some cheese. He'd often take that to work.

They found his piece box floating in the water when they drained the mine. It had his mark on it. He had a special way of writing his initials so that it looked like the 'A' was inside the 'D'. He had it scarted on just about everything that belonged to him. Even long after he was dead, I'd come across something, turn it over and there it would be, the little bowed out triangle with a line across the middle, and it would make me smile or cry. Billy Porterfield brought it to the door one teatime. Davie often worked with the Porterfields. My first thought was that they'd found Davie, and he must have known that by the look on my face because the first thing he said was we haven't found him yet, Jess, but we came across this floating in the water.

Well, it was corroded but you could just see Davie's mark on the inside of the lid. I didn't know if you'd want it or not, but I thought I'd fetch it to give you the chance. I wiped my hands on my pinny and took it from him. It felt rough and had a cold dampness about it. I looked at it and I looked at Billy standing there knowing that he might well have been dead himself because it was sheer luck that he wasn't down the pit the day of the Disaster. It had been his wife's mother and father's silver wedding the night before and he'd slept in. I smiled and thanked him for bringing it. I asked him how his mother and father were because he had two brothers still down the pit the same as Davie. He just shook his head. His father was kept busy with the mine and so was he but his mother had hardly eaten a thing in all this time. His youngest brother had only been fifteen, a cheery boy who would never pass you without saying a word. And the other one was just twenty-one. He'd been shaping up to be really good at quoits and a good runner too. He'd run in the local sports the Saturday before the Disaster. A lot of the miners had. You would often see them in the summer up the burn stripped to the waist and jumping over the water, jumping hennies they called it. I remember the first time I saw them. I was fascinated with what I thought were funny shaped tattoos but my father told me that was where they'd bashed themselves and the cuts had healed over with the coal dust inside. Davie never got any but then he wasn't working close with the coal. As often as not, he was on the ironstone and even then his job was to trundle it away from the face in a big hutch. He didn't handle it as much as those who worked with their picks and hammers. Davie said that sometimes the coal miners looked like flies trapped between slices of bread the seams were so narrow. And they'd be sweating so much that they'd have their shirts off; that's how they'd get all marked.

After I told Billy Porterfield to tell his mother and father I was asking for them, I took Davie's piece box into the house and laid it on the fender to get it dried out. I don't know what I thought I was going to do with it. It was no more than bits of rust hanging together. But I sat and looked at it and tried to rub the smell of it off my hands. Next thing I knew, Sadie was in. I'd been crying and I'd had no tea, and the tears started with Sadie when she saw what I was looking at. She'd come round to see if I'd heard that they'd more or less got the mine dry and should be able to get down into it in the next day or two. So I told her what Billy Porterfield had said when he'd fetched the piece box. We were pleased at the thought of them being able to find Davie and Johnny and the rest but at the same time our stomachs churned at the thought of what was in front of us, wondering what kind of state they'd be in. We gripped each other's hands and looked into the fire. Then Sadie got up to find me something to eat. She liked to see people fed. But did she not go and make me a sandwich. As soon as she brought it across she took one look at the box sitting on the fender and her face fell. She hadn't thought. I told her not to worry because I wasn't hungry although I did take a couple of bites to please her and we had a cup of tea. As we sat there we wondered daft things like whether or not they'd have eaten any of their pieces that day. And we wondered how long it would take before they found them all, if they would find them all, and what we would do if they didn't. Sadie was sure they would. There was no fire or water to hold them back now. But I was worried that maybe it had all collapsed in on itself, and I was right, some of it had.

I had a funny dream one night. Love had been drinking brandy and fallen asleep. I could see his dream; it appeared like a tableau beside him. A naked figure swung a pickaxe against a wall made of clotted blood. The most hellish flames circled the boy till his body turned to ebony and he fell at Love's feet. Love woke up crying out how could anyone let anything so cruel happen? Then he took hold of the dead miner's head and nestled it in his arms. I never usually remember my dreams but I remembered that one.

Martha: January 1890

Davie Anderson was down the pit when Martha was born. He went away in the morning as Helen's Dad and came back at teatime to find Martha all wrapped up in a shawl lying in a crib made out of the top drawer of the kitchen dresser. Martha's granny was there helping out, helping to look after their mother, and all she could say was that he'd not managed a boy yet but her Dad told Martha when she was older that he was never fussed for a boy – they were too much trouble. Her Aunty Nellie was there as well because it was a lot of hard work getting a baby. She was there fetching and carrying and making cups of tea. She'd been the first one to hand Martha to her mother and she told Martha that she'd never seen any woman as happy as when her mother had got a hold of her that first time. She'd gasped and said how bonny Martha was and that she loved her and Martha's Aunty said she'd never forget how her mother had fished in the blanket that was wrapped round her and put her pinkie inside Martha's hand. I love to see their little fingers she'd said. She'd still had some strength then. It was later on that she died, after they'd had to take her to the hospital because her waterworks went all to pot.

Not long after the New Year it was my birthday, the twelfth of January; I was eight years old. It was a Saturday so we'd no school and no church. It was cold, so cold the Tweed had frozen over and there was a bonspiel that day. We were allowed to go and watch because Big Alex was playing and he'd said that he'd keep an eye on us. So we got all wrapped up with mufflers and pawkies and overcoats. Tom brought an old tin with holes in that he'd stuffed with oily rags and had them smouldering away for us to warm our hands on. By the time we got down to the waterside, Big Alex was in the middle of his second game and he let loose a near-perfect shot just as we arrived; the stone birled to a stop right in the middle of the circle and knocked out two of the other team's stones into the bargain. He was playing for the railway workers, then there was the mill, they had two or three teams in, the smiddy, the shopkeepers, Dr Henderson and Mr Forsyth the lawyer with some of their friends. There were teams from Walkerburn, Traquair and Peebles, and, to our great delight, teachers from the school: Mr New, the headmaster, Mr Wilson, Mr Gunn, and Mr Mitchell the janitor. We all liked Mr Mitchell. When you first knew him, he could be scary. He'd been in the army and was good at shouting, but in the infants class we were allowed to go along to his room, well, it was a glorified cupboard, and get hot water for our cocoa. There would be quite a queue some days but he was always patient with us. His room was full of things to look at. There was the bell; it seemed huge and was heavier than it looked because, now and then, if he was in a good mood, he'd let us have a go at lifting it. All the cleaning stuff was in there: mops and pails, handy for if anyone spilled anything or wee'd themselves; a bag of sawdust for soaking up sick; and a first aid box. We weren't allowed to look inside that in case we got it dirty but we knew what was in it – bandages, iodine, wads of pink lint, safety pins – from all the skint knees we'd had dressed. There were blocks of soap all neatly stacked, rolls of string and a big snow shovel. The room smelled of carbolic mixed in with tobacco and damp clothes when it was wet or snowy because he dried out his jacket and his gloves at the side of the log burner in the corner. The urn sat on top of it and he'd dole out hot water with a flick of the wrist that always seemed too dainty for such a big man. My favourite thing in the room was his tea caddy. It sat on a shelf beside the stove along with an old bent spoon and a jar with milk in it. It was black and gold with a picture on the front of a man in a big hat fishing beside willow trees. Their branches dipped down into the water and a bird like a kingfisher sat on one of them, watching. Different days there'd be different stories about how he got it. One day he'd had to wrestle a Bengal tiger that was going to eat a maharajah's favourite child when he was out in India with the army and he'd got it as a thank you, another day he'd sailed into China on the fastest clipper on the seas and bought it off a Chinaman with a pigtail and a long silk shirt for a handful of malachy, and he'd pull a green stone with a pattern of circles on it from his pocket. We'd all stand there wide-eyed and open-mouthed as we hung on his every word. We knew that the stories weren't true but we wanted them to be true because we were always so thrilled when he told us one.

We always had great fun at the bonspiel. We'd find a piece of ice nearby and make slides. I loved sliding. I'd take a run up, launch myself onto ice that had been worn shiny and feel like I was flying. I loved it. I'd get so excited and desperate for my next turn I'd fall over in my hurry to get back in the queue. And the big ones would do fancy stuff. They'd hunker down or twirl round as fast as they could. They'd go down two at a time and end up in a heap at the far end with everyone laughing and shouting at them. By the end we'd all be getting gallus and doing something to please ourselves or make the crowd laugh. I thought I was the tops doing a little twirl at the end. Helen was too timid; she always just played it straight.

Phamie was good at going down on one leg, bent forward like a skater but Tom was the best. He'd be hunkered down, one leg stuck out like a Cossack dancer as he lifted his bonnet. He'd usually fall over and we'd all guffaw but now and then he'd manage to hold his position all the way down and there would be a big cheer. When we got too cold we'd go and get a heat at the braziers up on the banking. If you knew someone you might get a drink of tea from them. The Minister's wife was always good for that, she'd have brought extra cups and the Guild women would have done some baking. Grown-ups had to pay for their tea and cakes. The money would be used to send bibles to the heathen or to help homes for orphans. But as children we would always get something. The Minister's wife liked us because we weren't greedy. And I was pleased to see people spending their money that day because that's what I was now, an orphan. Although I was sick of hearing people whispering it whenever they saw me and Helen. It was as if their pity turned me into something that wasn't me. So sometimes I'd not speak to people who did that and I'd get a skelp on the ear from my granny if she was there or if someone told her about it. The school bullies still used it to torment us but we were learning not to rise to the bait. I was better than Helen; more often than not she'd just go red in the face and run away or burst into tears. But I found out that saying things like that at least my mother and father were married or at least my father had never been in the jail put their gas at a peep. It was a funny feeling just the same. I know we were lucky, if we could call it that, but the thought always made me think about the motherless things people brought to my grandfather, how shivery they were, and how they didn't know how precarious their life was.

I always had a special thought for my mother on my birthday. I'd imagine how she'd have looked, what she'd have been like, and I would speak to her often. Before I went to sleep I'd tell her what I'd been doing and what had happened to me and to Helen that day. Or I'd kid on I was the little girl in the story selling matches but that it was my mother that I saw and not my grandmother. I'd be so carried away with the story that I'd feel myself lift up off the ground and float up to heaven beside her. That would just be me falling asleep. But it felt so real that I'd be disappointed to wake up. Mind you in the winter I was glad to get up. I would lie there terrified, convinced, if I heard a noise outside, that Jack Frost was coming to nip my toes. I had to get up though. It was me and Helen's job to get the coal in and start the fire. We'd have brought the coal in from the coal bunker the night before; it would be all ready in a pail. Helen was in charge of setting the fire. I was the fetcher and carrier and the one that had to make the tea and take it through to my granny and grandfather. Mind you, that would be when we were older. But even so, from when we were anything we had our jobs to do about the house. On Friday nights we cleaned the cutlery: we scraped powder off a Bath brick onto a board and scoured anything metal then sharpened the knives with emery paper. We lifted the rugs and put down the Sunday ones for the weekend. We grated salt off the block and cleaned the brass ornaments. My granny liked collecting them. Some were fiddly to clean. There was a bell shaped like a crinoline lady with a skirt that took a hell of a lot of rubbing, and a tray-like thing that had a relief picture of a ship in full sail; many's the Friday night I cursed those sails. Helen and I'd take turns at cleaning the ornaments or the fender. We washed dishes, took the rugs outside and beat them, cut up papers into squares and put string through them for hanging in the toilet, swept and mopped, cleaned out cupboards – you name it, we did it. The older we got, the more we got to do. A right pair of Cinderellas we were but no fairy godmother for us. Nearest we had was Jess. I missed her when she died; the Spanish flu got her just after the war. It was her that got us away from our granny in the end. She would visit when she could and I think just knowing that was good. That and having Phamie's family nearby. As soon as each of us left the school we went to work in the mill but Jess had a cousin in Edinburgh who got Helen into service with a good family. That's where she met Billy Smeaton, he was the groomsman. She ended up living down in Ashington, in the north of England, when he got a job down there. Then a while later Jess got me fixed up with Henry Dobson the painter. He was born in Innerleithen. He'd been doing a painting for the family Jess's cousin worked for and said his wife could be doing with a girl to help about the house if she knew anyone. So the cousin sent word to Jess because she knew Helen was well thought of. I was lucky: decent folk, nice children, big house in Edinburgh, a whole different world. I was well-fed and had a room at the top of the house with a view across the water to Fife. I was the only servant although it just felt like I was there lending them a hand. It's not as if I wasn't used to housework, and the children were great fun. I wasn't left with them all the time. Mrs Dobson wasn't one of those kind that was glad to be rid of them. They knew who their mother was. Little Cowan was cute. He couldn't say Martha. Atta he called me, Atta. He ended up being a painter too.

Mr Dobson painted me. That was something I could never have imagined would happen. He said I had the loveliest complexion he'd ever seen. I ended up in two or three of his paintings. And they sold. He was getting more famous by the day. His stuff was popular. It sold well in the likes of Canada to people who'd emigrated. I suppose it would remind them of home.

Another new thing for me was doing so much washing. Small children don't half generate a lot of extra washing. When I'd been at home, the washing was about the only thing my granny always did herself because it was done on a Monday morning when were at the school, or working. But even so we'd help her get it in off the line when we came home, fold it up and put it away or air it off on the screen by the fire or the pulley that hung from the kitchen ceiling. And in the school holidays we'd take it in turns to turn the mangle. We'd dissolve the starch for the whites rinse and nip to the grocer's if she ran out of dolly blue. And we never ironed. She said she enjoyed it but it was more likely that she'd be worried we'd burn the clothes.

For the rest of my life work was never a hardship. Even when all the work was done and we were sitting by the fire at night often as not we'd be busy. We'd knit and sew: dishcloths, socks – I could turn a heel from when I was a young girl – mittens, hats and scarves for the winter, rag rugs, blanket strips with odds and ends of wool – the wool would be all colours, whatever the mill was selling off, and embroidery. My granny could turn her hand to any kind of sewing, knitting or crochet. Embroidery was what she liked best. It seemed to calm her down. She would get out her needle and threads and within five minutes her face would lose its pinched-up look. I've even heard her hum a tune. She taught me and Helen all the stitches that she knew and never shouted at us. She would even tell people how neat-fingered we were. I got called out to the front one time at the school to show my work to Mr Euman and Mr Smail when they did their inspection. They weren't the Inspectors from Edinburgh; they were on the school board and came round a few times in the year. I think they looked at the account books, the money, and checked that the staff were teaching us what they were supposed to be teaching. Mr Euman was the tailor. He had a shop on the High Street, on the other side from Smail the printer's.

I always liked the school, not surprising in that it took me out of the house. I started early, earlier than I should have. Tom and Helen came back every day with the greatest stories about playing chase in the playground, drawing, learning to read and to count, so that when Phamie went (she was just that bit older than me) I tagged along. My granny thought I was just going to the end of the road with them but I went right in to the school and was there until the teacher sent me home. But every school day morning I went along with Helen and Phamie and Tom till they got fed up of sending me away and asked my granny if she'd be happy for me to start. Which she was. That was me off her hands.

I loved the infants' teacher, Miss Robertson her name was. Many's the morning she'd get me to stand at the front and sing for her before the work started because I had such a sweet voice she said. When he was unwell, my grandfather liked nothing better than to have me sing to him while he lay in bed and drank his tea. I had quite a little repertoire that went from the holy through Rabbie Burns to the near bawdy! We learned Rabbie Burns at the school and I really took to songs like *My love is like a red red rose,* and *Ae fond kiss.* Even when I was wee, I could sense how full of feeling they were. I enjoyed the livelier ones too; the kind we would sing in a crowd round at Phamie's. My favourite was *Rantin, rovin Robin* because it was about a child that's born in January, same as me. Of course it was him, he was born in January; it was him that the blast o' Januar wind blew hansel in on. Sometimes there'd be a prize or a certificate. I got a certificate one year for singing *Flow Gently Sweet Afton.* And we had to learn the poems off by heart. We'd be up at the front of the class trying our best to put a bit of effort into it and liven it up. We'd guide our ploughshares then be aghast at knocking down the mouse's nest or the mountain daisy; we'd drive a dagger into that haggis and spill its entrails with such gusto that we might have been crazed murderers. Drawing was another thing I liked, not that I was much good at it. And I liked to be outside in the fresh air running about, playing tig or peevers. Skipping was my favourite, the kind with the big long rope and someone at each end to caw it. I was never so keen on going home. I was inclined to dawdle and how bad the dawdling was might depend on whether I knew what was for the dinner or the tea. Certain things would guarantee me home in a hurry: stovies; lentil soup; haggis, neeps and tatties. But there were things I wouldn't rush for: hare soup for one. I'd go hungry rather than eat it. It's made with blood drained out of the carcass that congeals in lumps if the broth's too hot when it's put in. There was something about the hare that made me not want to eat it. It felt different from a rabbit somehow. Rabbits were ten a penny but the hare, well you didn't see them too often and they seemed more wild and aloof, more knowing. I once saw one up Leithen, up on the hillside, in the snow; I couldn't get over how huge it looked, it must have been the angle I was at, or the light. I didn't like the thought of anyone killing them. Just like I couldn't bear the thought of any animal being trapped. I got that from my Dad. He never set a trap since the day he came across a young doe that had been caught by the leg; she'd just about chewed it off in her agony, and she was pregnant. He thought he was going to have to do something to put her out of her misery but she died right in front of him. It was the look in her eye that sickened him. At least with a fish, a quick dunt on the head and that was it. And he'd never kill a spider, shoo it outside maybe, but never kill it. Too good at catching flies he'd say. So I never killed a spider if I could help it even though they could make me jump, especially the huge ones that came into the house at the end of summer. I once knew a girl who was convinced they ate birds; she was a silly besom. Big Eileen we called her. She lived in the Toll cottage, just across from the Toll Wood. We played there a lot. It was great for building dens and the swings and there was a huge tree that was easy to climb. It had a comfy branch not that high up but high enough up to give you a different look at things. There are was a hole in the bark near where we sat that filled up with water and never really dried out; it had a funny smell that I didn't like but I'd always have to poke it.

We'd play hide and seek. One time Phamie was jumping with excitement when she found me because she'd spied a bird's nest in a bush and was desperate to show me it. We crept up to the bush and held our breaths as Phamie pulled back leaves and twigs. We saw three or four pale greeny blue eggs lying in amongst moss and down, and before we knew it, Phamie had lifted one out and we were all set to hatch it ourselves. I had it cupped inside both hands as we hurried back along the path to the road. We would keep it in a cardboard box in her Dad's greenhouse until it hatched then feed it worms and sugary water out of a dropper. We had it all planned out when we met Tom and the rest of the crowd all wondering where we'd been and what was I carrying. Well, Phamie could hardly get the words out quick enough to tell them about it and they were all desperate to see the egg, shouting at me to give them a look at it. So I opened up my hands to let them see when someone shoogled me. It fell onto the ground and smashed and there was the baby bird or what would have been one, a little featherless thing with closed eyes and a big head covered in watery stuff, in the dirt. I screamed and that's when Big Eileen appeared out of her house. Everyone was staring at the mess. Big Eileen threatened to tell our mothers, and seeing me, my granny. Well that made it worse. I was inconsolable. I got a row for being too quiet when I got home. You're too quiet – what's wrong with you? What have you been up to? I didn't dare say. I'd have got a leathering. Mind, that might have made me feel better, if I'd been punished for the bad thing I'd done.

Martha and Helen were up Caerlee hill. It was a summer's day. It was so warm that if they looked up the path they could see the heat shimmering a haze of wavy lines above it. The air smelled of warm dry grass, of sheep, bracken and wild thyme. It was so still and quiet that as they passed a gorse bush they heard the dry raps of its seedpods bursting open. They wandered off the main path looking for blaeberries and found some on the open hillside looking across to Traquair. The tiny purple berries stained their hands as they picked them. It did the same to their mouths and they giggled as they bared their ghost story teeth and made faces sticking out their blue black tongues. Then Helen noticed a rope lying on the grass about ten feet away from them down the hill. They ran down to find that it disappeared down a big hole that had been covered over with bracken and heather twigs. They shouted down, hello, but there was no reply. Together, they grabbed the rope and pulled hard. It felt as if there was no weight on the end of it. It glided up and out of the hole till Martha and Helen heard a bump near the edge. One last extra effort and out popped a cupboard drawer with a lamb in it. It's the Lamb of God said Helen, and went to lift it out.

Jess: Spring 1890

It took eight days to tunnel through the biggest fall. Hundreds of hutches of dirt they took away before they found anyone. They must have started on a Tuesday because it was the next again Wednesday when they came across the first bodies: a boy face down and the rest crouched against a wall. Davie was one of them.

I didn't envy the men who brought them out. The mine was dangerous and the sights they must have seen don't bear thinking about. Dr Badger, the town's doctor, who went about on a beautiful horse and kept his stethoscope in his top hat, said that the bodies were mummified. Mummified: that was the word he used. We'd hear all sorts we didn't want to hear: they were unrecognisable; fungus was growing out of them like moss on a dyke; their skin shrivelled up like a spider's web when it was touched; hair and beards just came away in the rescuers' hands. And well, we saw it ourselves when we had to.

As often as not it was only the clothes that could tell you who they were although the boy Dempster's father knew him by his bent finger. But one of the youngest Meikles was buried twice because they thought he was someone else and Jimmy Irvine lay for days before they realised it was him. It was a cruel week until we got them all out and buried. And for all we knew it was coming, we could never have imagined how it would be. It had been bad enough for those who'd had to cope with it the first time around, some of the bodies had been burned or bashed about, and there was the poor man Hunter who'd scraped his fingers to the bone. But trying to work out who was yours with them in that state – they weren't even the colour of human beings. The ironstone had seeped into everything and turned them all the same rusty red that had run down the burn when they'd pumped the water out.

You're never the same after you've seen the likes of that. And the smell, it stayed with me for days. They'd put something down on the floor to try and mask the smell, lime

I think it was, a white powder, but to me it just made it worse.

Seventeen they got out that first day. By the time I got up to Mauricewood there was a good crowd because there were still more than thirty missing and everyone was desperate to know who was out. There would be a shout – *a boy – not very big, buttoned waistcoat* – or – *big man, beard – think it might be so-and-so* – and you'd hear a gasp and there would be a murmur as people went forward to the shed that they'd set up for the bodies.

Half a dozen I looked at before I knew it was him. The first one was the worst. I got such a shock at the sight of the poor soul. I learned quick not to look too close at their faces or hands and I got to wondering how on earth I would know it was Davie. He had a small almond-shaped birthmark just under his left ear but I had a good idea I wouldn't be seeing that. And then I thought I would just know. But I didn't. At least twice the breath left me because I thought it was him only to realise it couldn't be. Then I reckoned I should look for his watch chain. He was pernickety about where he fastened it onto his waistcoat but then not many of them had waistcoats on, they'd taken them off to work. As it turned out, I didn't know him. There'd been a shout that they thought it was him because he wasn't very big but I said no, that couldn't be him; he didn't have a jacket like that. I think it was just self-preservation. I came out of the shed convinced but every step I took away from it I was less and less sure. There was something niggling so I went back in and got them to look at the soles of his boots. I asked if there was an extra seg on the heel of the right foot and there was. He must have got a jacket from someone else because he'd have been stripped to the waist, and right enough, when they got Dave Penman, he'd only his shirt and a waistcoat on.

I couldn't believe that was Davie. I just stood there shaking my head. The men in the shed were all sorry. They'd thought it was him and what did I want to do. Well I couldn't think,

I had to go away and find my mother. Sandy Dickson helped me outside. I don't really remember that much about the next wee while. I know my mother sorted things out with the men about getting Davie down to the house, that was after she'd cuddled me in and taken the worst of the sobbing against her shoulder. All I kept saying was that I couldn't bear it and she cooried me in like I was a child again. Then Sadie took over until I was strong enough to go back down to the house. They still hadn't found Johnny Glass.

It was Spring and the days were getting longer. The sun was trying its best to shine when I went down that hill from Mauricewood to Shottstown with my mother, and my sister too by this time. I winced every time it came out behind a cloud. I just wanted my eyes to stay shut. I just wanted not to be me, not to have to think about a funeral.

One of the first things I did was send word to Innerleithen that they'd got Davie out and that I'd let them know later about the arrangements. We knew the funeral would have to be soon. We thought maybe Friday and that was how it worked out. Seven of them were buried that day: Davie, Tommy Strang, Billy Wright, Jock Purves and Will Grieve that I can remember and I think maybe Jim Porteous and the lad McKenzie— I get muddled up. I had to get Davie's Minister because he belonged to the Parish Church, not that he was a big attender. He'd started coming along with me on a Sunday and spoke about lifting his lines but he hadn't so he was still officially Parish Church when he was killed. The Rev Jamieson, the Minister, had the gall to be a wee bit sniffy about it too. We've not seen much of David recently he said when he came to the house to see me about the funeral service. And I said no, that'll be because he's been buried half a mile underground for the last six months. My mother was affronted at me being cheeky to a Minister but I didn't care. Have you seen the state of them that they've brought out, Mr Jamieson? That quietened him. He was polite after that but never what you would call warm. Of course, I was Free Kirk and that didn't suit. You would get men in the mill that would barely look at folk who didn't go to their church. But they were few and far between. And Mr Crockett, well, he was such a character. I know for a fact that many's the Parish Church parishioner would rather have had him as their minister. I always remember Jeannie Brunton; Elsie Duthie invited her along on our summer trip and she enjoyed herself so much that she lifted her lines the next week. I never knew you could have so much fun with Kirky folk she'd said to Elsie. We'd had a super day out, right enough. It was one of the times we went to Peebles. It was that same year I buried Davie. We went by horse and cart, two hours to get there and another two back again and raining by the time we headed home but we'd had such great fun we couldn't have cared. It's a bonny place, Peebles, in among the hills, the Tweed right through the middle. It has some lovely shops and a wide, sunny High Street that's a pleasure to wander up and down. Davie and I often went there when we were courting. So we'd had a rake about and some of them went boating on the river up at Haylodge Park while the rest of us watched from the banking. I was in mourning so I didn't go in but I think I had the first inkling of things lightening that day. Once or twice I caught myself laughing and I hadn't done that in a good while. And I enjoyed my tea, something I hadn't done either for God knows how long. But the day out, the company, the fresh air all helped and I tucked into my ham salad good style. We'd booked into Lossock's Temperance Hotel and they'd done us proud. It was no wonder we converted Jeannie Brunton that day. She never regretted it. Too many people that think too much of themselves in the Parish Church she said to me once when we were at one of Mr Crockett's slideshows.

But I had to get Davie buried and I just had to be as civil as I needed to be to the Reverend Jamieson to get a decent job done. Not that we'd ever really spoken much about our own funerals but I remembered Davie saying that he'd like the hymn *I to the hills will lift mine eyes* because he loved being out on the hills, so the Minister seemed quite pleased with that. And it wouldn't have been a funeral without *The Lord's my Shepherd*. I made sure it would be the tune Davie liked because I wouldn't have liked to bury him to a tune he wasn't so fond of, so it was Crimond. My sister Chrissie sung her heart out. I couldn't sing a note so I was pleased to hear her voice so strong. And Davie's mother gave it everything. She'd brought the two girls; they stood one on either side of her. I didn't think it was right. They were far too young, but she was determined; he was their father and she was as sure as day that they were to see him put in the ground beside their mother. I thought it was cruelty, terrifying the two of them. Helen would be scarce ten years old and nervy at the best of times and Martha two years younger. I could see that Martha was taking it all in though. It was her that quieted Helen when they started to fling the dirt into the grave and she shouted out for her Dad. Davie's mother yirked her arm and told her to wheesht.

For a good job I'd said my own cheerios to him in the house before they came. I knew that once his mother arrived the day wouldn't be mine for long. She was good at suffering. She liked to be seen as the big martyr, left with two orphaned children and a man that couldn't work any more. I just let her get on with it. I kept my thoughts to myself and tried to keep a picture of Davie's smiling face at the front of my mind, tried to remember his voice telling me what bonny blue eyes I had and him singing, and hell, did the words of a song with a line about playing with breasts not come into my mind that I couldn't get rid of. I thought that's him doing that, being a mischief as usual. It was a song that Sadie used to sing to tease me when I first went out with him, *Doon the burn, Davie* it was called, about a courting couple that get carried away with themselves on a walk by the waterside. I had a quiet smile at that. Sadie was there for me at the cemetery although they still hadn't found Johnny. She'd sat with me before the funeral. I told her she didn't need to because she had the children, but her mother was there for them and, anyway, as long as she was with me she wasn't waiting for a knock at the door. And I enjoyed the company. I only had the coffin the one night. By the time they got themselves sorted out up at the pit it was the Thursday before they brought him down to the house. They'd found seventeen the first day, the Wednesday, a dozen on the Thursday, and then no more until the Monday.

It was the afternoon when they brought him home. I'd been in to my work in the morning to see about getting the time off and they were good about it. For all I knew what was coming, I never got over the shock of seeing that box in my house and all I could think was that he hadn't deserved this. I had a good cry once the men who'd brought him went away. They were so kind, so careful with the coffin. I started to thank them but I couldn't, my mother had to see them out.

I hardly had a minute till it was dark: neighbours in and out, Mr Crockett to see me. My mother went away to get my father's tea but she was coming back later to sit with me through the night. Sadie had come in while I was gathering together what I would wear to the funeral. I hadn't had much inclination to buy mourning clothes but between what I had and a few things that others gave me – my sister had a good black skirt that she'd got when her mother-in-law died, and my mother had brought me a short jacket that was just getting nippy on her – I was satisfied. I was busy looking for the cameo brooch that Davie had given me when we got married and that I wanted to wear when I heard the most terrible racket. I went through to the other room and there was Sadie hauling the bath tub out into the middle of the floor in front of the fire and the kettle and two pans on the boil. I thought a bath would make you feel a lot better able to face tomorrow she said. And for all I couldn't be bothered I knew she was right. We'll have you in and out before your mother comes back, and she ran back and forward with the kettle and the pans till she filled the tub. And see what I found in the cupboard she said, producing a glass bottle with a stopper. It was some rosemary oil that Davie'd got for rubbing into his scalp. I thought it might make the water smell nice. She poured some in and she was right enough, though its scent made me cry because it reminded me of how much I loved to watch him shave. He'd laugh at me and say I'd better stop or he'd lose his concentration and cut himself. He'd stand there in his vest peering into the mirror that hung above the wash stand and I'd be mesmerised as his face appeared out of the soap all tight and shiny. All I'd want to do was kiss it but he'd dare me to joogle him.

My tears started Sadie off. She helped me off with my clothes. At least you've got Davie out of there. What if they never find Johnny? And I said maybe that wasn't such a bad thing when you saw what had happened to them. Better just to remember him as he was. But she shook her head. I want him out of there, Jess. I want somewhere I can go where I know what's left of him is there for me to speak to, somewhere I can take a flower and sit and think about him, somewhere I can take the girls.

That bathwater was lovely. I've never had a bath like it before or since. I don't know if it was the smell, the not expecting it or that it was just what I needed, but it was delicious. And I said to Sadie, did she not want to jump in after me; it seemed a shame to waste the water and it wasn't as if I was

dirty. She laughed and said she supposed she might as well.
That kind of thing never bothered us. She just stripped off
and climbed in while I got dried. She sat back with her eyes
closed and slooshed the hot water over herself. We'll never
get our lives back, will we, Jess she said. We'll always be lost,
or a bit of us will. And I said that I couldn't see how it could
ever be any other way.

Earlier that day they found the ones who'd been with George
Muir the Overman. Their bodies were behind a stopping
built to hold back the smoke. They'd pulled up one of the
turntables and blocked up the holes with fireclay. The two
Meikle boys were in that lot, two of the youngest ones down
the pit, and Charlie Hamilton. The Meikles' father and
uncle were found with Davie. It was the uncle whose flask
had writing scratched on it. That wasn't a good thing to hear
about; it meant that there must have been time for him to
write it, that we'd been right all those nights when we tortured
ourselves about them waiting for somebody to come and
rescue them. They must have been alive when the pit was
sealed on the Saturday of Hugh MacPherson's funeral. What
the hell must have been going through their heads? I prayed
to God that they just faded away as the air gave out, that they
died still hoping they'd get out. They said they found some
of them sitting up against the walls and in some ways that
was a comfort. It made me think that they'd waited quietly
for death. Not like the poor souls they'd found in September,
the ones who had been nearer the fire and who they'd had to
pull out of holes and out from under anything that might have
given them some respite from the smoke.

Bill Brockie, the Colour Sergeant in the Royal Scots
Reserves, was found that day too and the two Porterfield
lads. The Porterfields were buried along with all four Meikles
on the Sunday in the old cemetery. The Saturday had seen
I can't remember how many buried – the most of them that

they found on the Wednesday and Thursday including two of the Dempsters and the laddie Brown who was meant to be married the day after the Disaster. Such a shame, you'd see his girl wandering about the woods half dead looking. Old man Dempster had come through from Linlithgow and only knew his son because of his bent finger. Two sons he'd lost and a grandson. Sandy Dickson told me they felt so sorry for him that they'd cut a button off his son's shirt for him to take home. He'd wrapped it up tight in his handkerchief, put it in his breast pocket and said this would be the end of him and his wife.

Bill Brockie's was an impressive funeral although he wasn't buried till the Monday; full military honours they gave him. Soldiers carried him on their shoulders all the way from Shottstown to the cemetery and a company of them followed behind his family and his friends. Pipers played *Land o' the Leal* at the graveside: that had me in tears; Bill Brockie had been a good friend to Davie when he'd started down the pit that last time, made sure he was in with a good squad; nobody in it that would craw.

Hutches were filled with coal and a wooden pin or tally attached unique to each worker. An unscrupulous miner might substitute his own pin or tally on a hutch which had been filled by another but the stigma of having been discovered doing such a despised act lasted many years.

If a hutch was unusually heavy, a suspicious check weighman would tip the contents out at the surface. All stone added to boost the weight would be weighed separately and this amount deducted from the weight of every subsequent hutch sent to the surface by that miner during his shift.

The offender's name was chalked up on a board at the surface for all to see, together with the weight of stone found, indicating that the miner in question had crawed – an old Scots word meaning inferior coal. This ignominy served as a deterrent to any workmen with similar ideas.

1

Thomas Meikle was a much esteemed and prominent member of the Plymouth Brethren. His wife had a feeling that if any time had elapsed between her husband's discovery of his danger and his sinking into unconsciousness, he was likely to utilise it in leaving a message for his loved ones.

So she asked one of the search party to pay particular attention to Thomas's flask. It was found in his pocket. However, the bottom had disintegrated and the upper part broken off. Rust had eaten most of what was left but it did seem as if there was a message.

This looked as if it had been scratched out with a pin and was deciphered using two powerful magnifying glasses lent by Mr Cowan of Beeslack. Five words appeared plain enough. These were, "for,"... "From,"... "Alexander,"... "God,"... and "Dying." Alexander was Thomas's middle name and that of his second-youngest son.

Plymouth Brethren have no official clergy or liturgy. They meet together as brothers and eschew church law in favour of grace. Thomas was the father of five children, aged thirteen, ten, eight, five and two: Margaret, Jessie, Isabella, Alexander and Thomas. A child's sock was found in his pocket.

6 15

I was on my way home from Bill Brockie's funeral when I met
a cart bringing a coffin with the body of Matt Wright in it.
They must have just flung him in and carried him straight
down the road. Bob Tolmie said that they'd found three in the
sump when they'd emptied it. When I heard that, I didn't half
scoot up that hill. I knew that Sadie had gone up earlier when
word had come round that they'd found the Kinninmonts
from Roslin, the son just fifteen and lying with his head on
his father's knee. That had us all hoping that they'd not be
long finding the rest.

When I got up to the pithead there was a fair crowd. I found
Sadie with Johnny Davidson's wife. They were the only two
that hadn't got their men. They held onto one another and
looked so hurt, as if they couldn't understand why they were
still there. Sadie just shook her head when I asked about Johnny
so I cuddled her into me and asked who else they'd found.
Wee Mitch Hamilton was one; his body had been in an awful
mess, not helped by them having had to use grappling irons to
fish him out, and Geordie Pennycook. Right enough, I'd seen
Lizzie Pennycook's children playing when I'd come through
the yard. She'd already buried her oldest in September, just
fourteen he was. When they'd shouted for her to go in to the
shed she'd handed over the baby to her neighbour. The word
was that she'd recognised Geordie's tobacco box, his boots
and the neck of his shirt, then collapsed.

We were just about to give up for the day when the shout came
that they'd found the last two. It was about teatime. Sadie
gripped my arm and asked if I'd go in with her. I could feel
her shaking. The lassie Davidson shouldn't even have been
there. She should have been in Australia. The whole family
had been packed up and ready to go, sold all the stuff they
weren't taking and all set to go the week after the Disaster.
Johnny Davidson had finished at the pit the weekend before,
only went down that day to make a few extra shillings before

they went. He was one the Company would've been glad to be rid of. He wasn't backwards at coming forwards to tell them their mine wasn't safe. He kept a map of the workings in his pocket just in case there was ever a fire. Fat lot of good it did him apart from taking him the furthest away from the heart of it. He'd taken Sadie's Johnny with him.

So the three of us went in to that stinking place for the last time. You got used to what they looked like once you got over the first shock, but that smell, there was nothing you could do to stop yourself heaving. I've never smelled the like since. Now and then maybe on a hot summer's day when the cart from the killing house goes by it reminds me but even then it's a pale imitation. This was far more hellish; it had a cold, heavy mouldiness about it that was choking. And, well, I've told you how Sadie knew which one was Johnny Glass. I shouldn't have let her look at his face. I always regret that. But she wouldn't have it any other way. I should have known when they had it covered like that that it wasn't going to be pretty. No wonder her legs gave way. It was all I could do to hold her up. Good job the men were there to help me get her outside. Johnny Davidson's wife didn't need to look for anything. It couldn't have been anyone else. But I was glad when one of her neighbours ran up to see if she needed anybody because she'd no one else with her. I had visions of having to take both of them home.

Johnny was buried the next day, Tuesday, along with Geordie Pennycook and Jimmy Irvine, him that lay for days unrecognised. Jimmy's wife didn't have her sorrows to seek that year. She lost her youngest in the July, just a year old.

They weren't such big funerals as the ones we'd had at the weekend. Well, there weren't so many to bury for a start. They'd taken four out of one house on Saturday, the three Dempsters and Willie Brown. All four of them went in the same hole. The other two that were buried on the Saturday were at Glencorse, Mitchell Hamilton, the father and his son, Charlie. They were Brethren and they had a short service at the pit head before they took them away. Then on the Sunday, the crowds were back to watch. They lined the streets for the funerals of the Porterfields, the Meikles, the Millar boy that they thought they'd already buried, and Tommy Hunter; he was another one that went straight to the cemetery from the pit head. Then on the Monday we had the soldiers out for Bill Brockie. By the Tuesday when we buried Johnny Glass, everybody was wearying. We'd been burying for four days straight and still it wasn't finished.

On Saturday 29th March a large number of people had congregated around the house at six, Lindsay Place, Shottstown, where the scene was an impressive one as the coffins of the three Dempsters and their neighbour, William Brown, were reverently placed in the hearse amidst the sobs of the women.

Robert Dempster was 37 when he was killed along with his unmarried younger brother and the eldest of his six sons. His body was discovered on the 25th of March 1890 beside that of his son. Three weeks before this, on 5th of March, his daughter, Robina, had been born.

It was as if they had gone as far as they could till it was no use. Robert Dempster and his son looked as if they were asleep, but when rescuers touched Robert's big black beard it came away in their hands and they were all very careful after that.

The boy Dempster had belonged to the First Penicuik Company Boys' Brigade. His cap and belt were placed on the coffin, while former comrades followed his remains to the grave. The chief mourner was his grandfather who was sore affected as all four bodies were placed in the same grave.

6 15

Mitchell Hamilton's mother was four months pregnant when he was entombed in Mauricewood with his father, also called Mitchell, and younger brother. She buried her husband and 14-year-old son on 29th March 1890. Mitchell was found on 31st March. Her baby was born on 2nd April. She named him Mitchell.

Charles Hamilton was fourteen and described as a pumper on the official list of persons in Mauricewood when the fire was discovered. His body was found on the same day as he was interred with his father at Glencorse churchyard. Glencorse Old Parish Church helped inspire Robert Louis Stevenson's *Kidnapped*.

Stoppage of the pumping engines had caused water to collect at the bottom of a declivity. So deep in this sump was Mitchell Hamilton's body that even the glare of search lanterns couldn't reach him and it was grappling irons which brought to the surface his poor little wasted body.

Mitchell Hamilton had raised the alarm. Sparks were flashing under the enginehouse door. Robb, the bottomer, opened it and saw flames in the pipe upset. He'd shouted to Hamilton, William Urquhart, and Robert Tolmie to run and warn the men, which they willingly did knowing the dangers only too well.

6 15

James Somerville was eighteen and a roadsman. He lived with his widowed mother, Mary, in Shottstown. His body was mistakenly identified as David Kinninmont and conveyed to Mrs Kinninmont's house in Roslin. Although not the body of her son, it was carefully dressed and watched until he was known.

Mistakenly identified as Robert Kinninmont and returned to Robert's family, James Somerville, a roadsman, was then thought to be twenty-one-year-old Martin Morgan, who was single and worked as a drawer. Martin's sister and several others walked out to Roslin where they recognised him. Martin was not found until March 1890.

Mrs Kinninmont had no news of her husband, David, or her son, Robert, until Monday 31st March, 1890. They were the first of the last seven bodies recovered. The rescuers came upon them at the top of the wheel brae at the end of the double lie in the west workings.

David Kinninmont was forty-five and his son Robert fifteen. They lived at Pearson's Cottages in Roslin. Two of the last to be buried, they had been found together and were interred on Thursday, 3rd April, 1890. Mrs Kinninmont was left with a son, Andrew, twelve, and a daughter, Davina, eight.

6 15

I think Sadie was relieved there wasn't such a big crowd for Johnny. To my mind you don't turn up at a stranger's funeral with the best of intentions. You're there to gawp at other folks' misery. And Love wasn't there this time. I'd told him he wasn't welcome at Davie's funeral when I saw him waiting in the crowd by the cemetery gates. It had made me feel better at the time but the change that came over his face when I said it still bothers me. But it was good to see folk from the town there.

It was a quieter service with the same Minister as buried Davie. He was such a po-faced, sanctimonious creature. I concentrated on making sure Sadie was all right – me and her mother between us. Her brother and sister-in-law were there too; come out from Portobello. And some of Johnny's family had managed to get to the funeral. His mother and father were dead but he had a brother in Leith and a nephew who was a piper; Wull his name was. He'd been brought up as Johnny's brother because his sister had had him when she was just fourteen. Young Wull had learned to play the pipes in the Army. When he played the *Floo'ers o' the Forest* at the graveside, that was one of the most heartbreaking things I've ever heard. I kept a tight hold of Sadie and looked hard at the wreaths while the Minister said his piece. There was one there from the Misses Cowan. They were good-hearted people, took after their father, Sir John. He owned the Valleyfield Mill where I worked. A well-known and well-loved man for all he was the boss. He'd help anybody out and he was involved in all sorts in the town – the Bank, the Kirk, the Volunteers, the local reform school at Wellington, the courts, the Liberals, and none of it any bother to him. He told the Disaster Fund Committee time and time again that they weren't paying out enough but oh no, those who were in charge of the purse strings were determined that nobody should be better off than they deemed necessary. And he was proved right. There was more than half of it left at the end when they stopped paying out. He had a lot of sympathy for people because he knew himself what it was like to lose someone. Twice he was made a widower and he'd lost three of his own children to the fever. We were all very sad when he died. He'd be well into his eighties. The old Queen was still alive, but only just. I wasn't surprised to see thousands turn out for his funeral at Glencorse. The two daughters he had left never married but were well liked in their turn. They sent a wreath to every single one of those who were lost at Mauricewood – and not just a small one. And well you might say they'd have been better giving people the money for clothes or hot dinners, but, I don't know. It meant that no matter what, every family had a memory of something beautiful to hold onto because there wasn't much else, and it made those who had lost somebody feel that they were worth something. Everyone was dignified by them.

At Davie's funeral, the flowers helped me hold myself together. I remember wondering what some of them were. I knew a chrysanth when I saw one or a carnation but there were others that I wasn't so sure of. They were waxy, bell-like some of them. I suppose they must have been lilies or jasmine; they had a heady scent.

As the *Floo'ers o' the Forest* played for Johnny Glass, I realised that was us nearly done with it all. We'd got them out and buried; we'd done our best by them. But I couldn't help but feel that the next wee while wouldn't be easy. I pushed that to the back of my mind though. I'd plenty to think about with Sadie, doing all I could to help at the tea in the house after. You'd hardly credit it, Johnny had only been found the night before, but Sadie's mother had set to and baked and so had her friends and some of the neighbours. I was able to bring things that I had in the house, and my mother brought some bramble and apple cordial that my father had made and that we'd had on Friday night, so that between us all there was plenty.

I'd sat up with Sadie as we watched Johnny on that last night he was ever in the house and it's a funny thing how you can find yourself laughing when you start to remember things. Not that there weren't tears but it was good to speak about their life together. Like the time not long after they were married when Johnny came to home to find her sobbing because she'd burnt the tea and they ended up with saps. She was good at burning things. She burnt a big hole in his good shirt; she'd left the iron too long on the fire. For a good job the hole was in a bit that was covered by his waistcoat. Then there was the famous time when she decided to get all dolled up for him one Saturday night when they were going out to a party, this must have been before the girls were born. She'd got a loan of a set of hair tongs from Enid Scott who worked beside her in the mill, and, oh, she was going to be so fancy with her hair all curled up, she'd even bought a new ribbon, but she let the tongs get too hot and burnt a big chunk right in the middle of her head at the back, burnt her scalp into the bargain; she never had any patience. She had to wear her hair up in a bun for a good long time until it grew back in again. Johnny would bother her about it; call her Cinders.

You always got the feeling that Johnny Glass was a boy who could have made a lot more of himself if he'd had the chance. I think that's how him and Davie got on so well. You couldn't be stupid and play cards the way they did. But Davie was a bit deaf and I think that's how he'd not done so well at the school. As for Johnny, his family moved about so much that he'd hardly ever be at the same school more than five minutes, then into the mine as soon as he was old enough. His father had been a mason's labourer so they'd had to move where the work was. Most of the time they'd been in about Edinburgh or Newtongrange but Johnny was born in Lauder down in the Borders and his oldest brother in Lochmaben.

There would be a lot of those who were down that pit

that never had a chance. The likes of the boy Sinnet, one of the first ones they brought out. He'd only started working a few days before. When I think about him sitting there in the dark working a big fan, I feel so vexed. At least he'd had some life. It wasn't so long before Mauricewood that children and women were going down the mines. Old Betty Smith worked down the pit as a child in the thirties before they put a stop to it. She worked in the mill when I knew her, in despatch, and if things were slack she'd be sent up beside us. Many's the time I've heard her speak about what it was like down the mine, what it was like to be so hungry that she'd steal a chunk of the horses' pease bannock or strip the bark off the trees on the way home. A bit dry bread or a cold potato was about as much as she ever got to keep her going. She hauled coal bent double along underground roads and up ladders. By the time she was twelve she could carry loads near a hundredweight. The baskets they used came right up over the neck. There was one miner took great pleasure in thumping the biggest lumps he could find onto Betty's back. She hated him. She was never so pleased as on the day he ruptured himself clearing some boulders.

She told us about children who could be down the pit at all hours of the day and night, hungry, hardly able to stand far less work, who, if they fell asleep, would get a dunt with a shovel or a pick handle. She'd seen a good few get their legs crushed; her own brother lost an eye when a spark off a pick went into it; he couldn't work for a year. And the places they worked would often be damp or running with water. Twice, her own mother had typhoid fever.

Betty was one of the ones they spoke to when there was the big Commission to investigate the mining industry. That was long before my day but people still spoke about it because it was such a big change when they stopped the women and children going down: a lot of people were a hell of a sight worse off. They'd lose a good two or three wages and no less mouths to feed.

There was one thing Betty could never get over: the people who did the asking seemed more interested in whether she could answer questions on the Shorter Catechism – and there were over 100 of them – than in whether or not the work made her unwell or even whether or not she could read or write. The Shorter Catechism! When you think about it, what good was being able to spout about the Trinity going to do the poor creatures that were taken down a mine with no say as to whether they wanted to or not? The government must've been worried. They'd be worried that if the workers weren't afraid of God they might not be afraid of them, they might not know their place, and then we might end up like they did in France.

Not that Penicuik can complain about the French. What a fancy job they made of building the houses on Bridge Street. They hadn't done it out of generosity. It was prisoners of war from when Napoleon was on the ran-dan who built them. Their barracks were in some of the old mill buildings. There's a French prisoner's tree just down the water from the mill. They were allowed to walk out that far, and as long as they came back again everything was fine. Mrs Crockett's auntie had seen Napoleon. He was on the south coast, on a Navy ship all set to take him to Elba. Small boats ferried people out to look at him. That was one of those things you got at the school: Able was I, ere I saw Elba; a line that reads the same both ways. Mind you, I could never work out what anybody was meant to be able for once they'd seen Elba. I suppose it's an island down in the Mediterranean Sea. Maybe that's enough to cheer anyone up. And of course Davie, any time Napoleon was mentioned, he'd be saying things like, aye, he was able for anything once he'd seen his elbow, or, he must have had a very grand elbow that Napoleon, he was able for anything once he'd seen it. That's the kind of thing we were having a smile to ourselves about when we sat and watched Johnny Glass the night before we buried him. I suppose there's many wouldn't have approved but they weren't there.

Come the morning I got the kettle going again. It had never been off the go all night. But we were sick of tea. You could have sailed a ship on the amount of tea we'd drunk. So I poured us both a brandy, I put a good drop of water in it, mind, and we sipped at that before we made a start.

That was the Tuesday. I went back to work on the Thursday. I slept near all day on the Wednesday. But by the Thursday I felt better able so away I went. It turned out that the Inspectors had gone down the mine the day we buried Johnny. That was the first of them getting anywhere near the workings. There was a crowd of them went down: the Inspector, one of the head people from the Company with his lawyers, along with two or three for the miners. By all accounts they didn't go very far, then they interviewed Love and two of the men who'd cleared the mine. It made no difference to what they came out with. We never thought it would. Still no blame laid where it was due. And by the time the Report came out they'd found the other stopping further in; four feet thick it was, four feet, and airtight, a shovel lying beside it.

In 1842 R. F. Franks reported to the Children's Employment Commission on the East of Scotland District. In Tranent, working children, miners, mine owners, local business men and clergy were interviewed. Interviewees were given a number and comments might be added as to their state of health, appearance, and education.

No. 173. *David M'Neil*, 9 years old, putter:
I've worked three years wi' Johnnie Scott. Father first carried me down. Father is dead. Mother takes my wages. I get my licks when I no like work. Mother gives me porridge and sour milk when am no well; am no very strong.

No. 158. *James Neil* aged 10 years, coal-hewer:
Been below 18 months; the work is gai sore. Place of work is not very dry. Never got hurt, but the work has given me piles, which pain me when I sit.
[Can read and write a little; knows a little Scripture history.]

No. 165. *Catherine Landels*, 12 years old, coal-bearer:
Works 12 hours and 14 hours daily.
Am much overworked.
Gets no regular meals; and change my clothes when no fatigued.
[Reads a little; just learning to make the strokes in the copy-book. Knows a few of the questions in the Shorter Catechism.]

8

No. 159. *William Martin*, 10 years old, coal-putter:

I fall asleep sometimes when we canna get the coals away, but the shaft of my father's pick wakens me.

My place of work is wet; the water covers my shoe-tops.

[Can sign his name, very much behind in the Catechism and Testament.]

No. 160. *William Kerr*, 11 years old, coal-bearer:

Carries coal on my back. Can fill a basket of 5cwt in six journeys.

I am o'er sair gone at times, as the hours are so long and the work gai sair.

[Went to school once; reads very badly; no scriptural knowledge whatever.]

No. 163. *John Martin*, 11 years old, coal-hewer:

Been 18 months at the coal wall. Cannot say I like it muckle.

Have not been to school since wrought below. Could write some, can put down my name.

Have had typhus twice and so has mother.

[Reads very well; been awfully neglected.]

No. 164. *Catherine Meiklejohn*, aged 12, coal-bearer:

It takes me three burthens to fill one tub of 5cwt. My back is very sore at times, but I never lie idle.

Mother is a coal-bearer.

[A most intelligent, healthy girl. Few men could do one-third labour this lassie is compelled to perform.]

8

I was in the Kirk the next Sunday; it was Easter. The Minister read the bit about Jesus telling Mary Magdalene not to touch him. All I could think was that I'd never touch Davie again, that I could see no consolation even in him rising from the dead. I broke down. I did my best to hold it in but I couldn't. I ran outside not caring if I made a fool of myself and sat on a wall as the pain of it all ripped through me till my mother and Chrissie came to find me.

Following the disaster Mr John Love was responsible for all reconstruction. A new second incline was built, three times the statutory size, fitted with a winding engine and carriages running on a fish-jointed railway between the surface and the lowest workings. All underground steam pipes and pumping engines were replaced.

A Waddle ventilating fan at the mouth of this incline exhausted foul air and drew in a supply of fresh air so abundant that only a small portion of it could be circulated to the workings as the current would have otherwise extinguished the naked lights used by the miners.

This expensive restoration indicated that the Company anticipated working the minerals for many years. However, the pit was closed in 1897: there had been another fire in February; the cost of maintaining sixteen ponies for haulage was too great; cheap Spanish imports affected profitability. By May, machinery was being removed.

Men were already leaving and finding employment elsewhere when closure was hastened by the dropping of a pump section weighing two tons which wrecked everything in its way after its supporting chain broke and it fell to the bottom of the mine. The pit was finally closed on 25th June.

1

Martha: March 1890

They found my Dad in the March, the end of March. They found him on the Wednesday or Thursday and the funeral was to be on the Friday. My granny hoyed us on the train and took us back up to Penicuik to be there. We hadn't much time to think about it. We'd got the fright of our lives at the school the day before when word came for me and Helen to go to the headmaster's office because that usually meant trouble. But I knew, when I saw Helen, it couldn't be that. Her face was white and I could see that she was close to tears. It was me who knocked on the door. We could hear voices speaking behind it and there, when we went in, was our granny in her best clothes and her hat with the black veil. The headmaster said come in, girls; your granny's got news for you. And no ceremony or breaking it to us gently she just said quite matter of fact, although her voice was strained, as if held in very tight, they've found your Dad and the funeral is tomorrow. We're going home now and I've arranged it with Mr New that you'll not be here then because I'm taking you with me. And looking at Mr New she said I think it's only right that they should pay their last respects to their father; there's nothing else we can do for him now. And Mr New said well, girls, I'm very sorry for your loss. You will need to be strong for your grandmother tomorrow. You can be a comfort to her and your grandfather as well as to each other. And then, I remember this as clear as day, before he opened the door for us to go out, he bowed to us. Don't ask me how I moved. When I'd heard my granny saying the words I didn't want to hear, my insides had turned somersaults and my legs turned to marshmallow. But I didn't say a word. Neither did Helen. We didn't dare. We collected our bags and our coats. Everyone stared at us, wondering what was going on. The likes of Peggy Simmonds whispered and sniggered behind their hands until Miss Lillie gave them such a look. Then never a word spoken until we got home where my grandfather was sitting in his chair looking lost saying, Aye, ma lassies, it's a rum do. He was dead within the year. It was as if he gave up. He hadn't been well for as long as I could remember but he'd always made an effort. Now he took to his bed and lay for months. Me and Helen helped my granny look after him. We'd take his food in on a tray and have a blether, or if he didn't feel up to eating we'd make saps: warm up some milk and pour it over bread sprinkled with sugar; he liked plenty sugar. And he loved to hear me sing. Send Martha in he'd shout to my granny and in I would go. *Flow Gently Sweet Afton* was a favourite of his and if my granny wasn't there I'd sing a favourite of mine about dancing in the woods and running away with the gypsies, doing all the actions; that cheered him up.

He went quick in the end. He'd been sleeping a lot and struggling to get his breath but we weren't expecting him to go when he did. It was me that found him. I went into the room with some fresh glycerine, his lips were cracked and we'd been dabbing that on them, laid it on the bedside cabinet and said how are you today, pa? But there was no answer. So I shook him. Pa, I said come on, waken up. But he wouldn't, so I shouted to my granny and she burst in roaring about the racket I was making till she saw him and the colour drained from her. She took him by the shoulders. Wullie, Wullie, she laid her head on his chest, you can't leave me. But he had. My mouth must've been hanging open because she chased me from the room and all I could think was that he couldn't be dead because he was a funny yellow colour, not wax white like Mary Queen of Scots.

My granny had always been one to hang about the sick. She would visit, do shopping, take cakes she'd made or bowls of bone broth. Plenty folk said what a kindly, godly woman she was but after my grandfather died she took to worming her way in so that she could sit beside the deathbed. She'd let the family have a night's sleep, insist nobody should be by themselves when they died. People got sick of her; called her the angel of death behind her back until Jim McNaught told her to get away back home, she had two lassies that needed looking after. It's no wonder I'm wary of charity. I always find myself thinking how many's the devil that comes with a do-gooding face.

Not much was said going up in the train. Big Alex had seen us into our seats and given me and Helen a pandrop each. Now be good, he said and look after your granny, and tell Jessie (he always called Jess, Jessie) that we're all thinking about her. Your Dad was a good man, it's hard enough to lose anyone but when they're like Davie, it's a lot harder. My granny closed her eyes and nodded. Big Alex said that he'd look in on my grandfather later on when he finished, keep him company for a while until we got home. Thanks, Alex, that would be good of you, my granny said and then we were off.

It was that time of the year when you start to feel that the winter's past and I remember thinking that I didn't want it to be past, I didn't want it to be the spring or the summer because it would be a spring and summer with no Dad in it. And all I could think about, going up in that train were happy times like last summer when him and Jess had come down to the Games. The people of Innerleithen liked to tell everybody that they were the oldest Games in the country, named after St Ronan because he was their patron saint. The story goes that he came across from Ireland with St Columba, caught the Devil by the hind leg up the Leithen and flung him out (or drowned him, one or the other). That's the story anyway and Sir Walter Scott used it in his book called *St Ronan's Well*. Not that I've read it.

My Dad liked to come down for the Games. Often he knew people who were running because a lot of the miners liked to keep fit and a good few of them played quoits. The man who won the quoits competition that year worked in the pit beside my Dad and was killed in the Disaster. George Livingstone his name was, one of the best in Scotland.

The Games were held on the Green just below the Nurseries. We had a great day that year, warm and sunny, and me and Helen were with my Dad and Jess, glad to get out of my granny's way. Most of the town turned out, even those who weren't much interested in the sports, because it was a day when you met people you maybe didn't see very often and wandered about in your Sunday best speaking to this one and that, watching a race or two. I never liked to get too close to the runners. They scared me, all that puffing and blowing as if they were about to burst with all the energy they put into each stride. My Dad put a bet on the favourite in the big race, our granny wasn't to know that though, then we sat down on the grass to watch the quoits.

There were miners there from Penicuik that my Dad knew and my uncle, my Dad's youngest brother (I suppose he'd just be a boy then – about fifteen or sixteen) who had a job in the bakers up in Penicuik and stayed with my Aunty Nellie and Uncle Bob. And there were a couple of my Dad's cousins from Peebles there too with their families. Me and Helen and the other children were kept busy fetching beer and lemonade from the marquee. I loved going into the marquee, it felt huge. I liked having the grass for a floor and the way the light came in through the canvas. Everyone was nice to us. They thanked us for bringing the drinks, told my Dad what pretty girls we were, bought us lemonade, gave us sweets, and my Aunty Nellie shared out some home-made treacle toffee. Someone else had brought a pie so that was shared out too. My Dad said how it was a smashing change from sandwiches and all the miners agreed. One of the children asked if they had a favourite sandwich and for most of them it was bacon, because that was tasty and a treat, but most agreed that cheese was the best all-round because it kept well and it filled you up; most of them took it with jam or lemon curd. Some put toast in beside their sandwiches to keep them fresh. There was one man whose favourite was a bar of chocolate between two slices of bread – a bar of chocolate. He must have seen my face because he said oh, aye, it's really good and even better when it's been down the mine for a good while; sandwiches take on a different flavour altogether when they've been down there. He said that when he got home, his children were always hoping that he'd not eaten them all so they could get a taste. Then my Dad told the story that I'd heard umpteen times before about Wull Dodds, an old miner that he'd known when he first started, sitting one day at dinner time. Wull had opened his sandwich box, made a face at the first sandwich and said cheese in a disgusted voice, then swore when he picked up the next one because it was cheese too, and my Dad had said to him can you not to have a word with your wife, Wull, if you don't like cheese? Wife, he'd snorted, I make my sandwiches myself. That always made my Dad laugh, no matter how often he told it.

They cheered on their pal in the quoits competition. By the time he landed the winner, the whole crowd of them were on their feet clapping and whistling, shouting, Well done, Doddie! When he wasn't playing, the chat was lively. All the miners teased Jess about working in the paper mill. They called her a mill dumper. Mill workers were soft as far as the miners were concerned, they had it easy and they didn't make so much money either. But Jess gave as good as she got. Penicuik paper was the best in the world, she said. It went all over and was good enough that they made banknotes with it. And the work could be dangerous. She knew a girl who was pulled into machinery by the hair and scalped, and Sadie's cousin's man was cleaning out a big tub with blades in the bottom that was used to mix the paper pulp when someone switched it on. Then there was that stupid man who fell into a big tank of boiling water when he'd tried to wash his overalls in it. And at least, she said, the mill workers don't go about fighting and carrying on like some of the miners in Shottstown. There

were two families in one of the streets near where Jess and my
Dad lived who had a rammy every Saturday night when the
pubs shut. Jess had looked out the window the weekend before
last and saw two of them stripped to the waist with knives in
their hands. Tinks the bloody lot of them, my dad said, they
don't know any better, think they're still in the peat bogs. He
stuck up for the miners though, said he'd known plenty in the
mill that were no saints; told them about the man he'd worked
beside who went home from the pub one Saturday night and
ate the stew that his wife had cooked for the family's Sunday
dinner, ate the whole lot, and worse, sicked it up five minutes
later, and the man who worked in the pay office who collected
his son's wages every week along with his own and drank it
all – with his pal to help him. That got them blethering about
some of the characters who went about Penicuik: the old man
who kept owls, who always went about with at least two of
them, one on each shoulder, and often one of them would be
on his head, its claws stuck into his bonnet; the fine-looking
German gypsy who came every year with a dancing bear on
the end of a chain; the man with no fingers on his left hand
because he chopped them off with an axe so that he couldn't
work; and Ecky the Tub, a cheery soul and not scared to
work, just not the brightest. He pushed a barrow round the
mill collecting the waste. The story went that one day they'd
got him inside a wooden tub and told him that they'd buy him
drink for a year if he could lift the tub while he was standing
in it. Well of course he couldn't. They had him training and
doing all sorts to build up his muscles and every week he'd
have another shot. I don't know how long that went on for.
Another time he'd been pushing his barrow across the mill
lade when a man standing at the mill gate, who could throw
his voice, had shouted Ecky the Tub. Ecky had turned round
and it just looked like the man was busy reading a notice that
was stuck on the gatehouse door. But when the voice came
again, he fell right in the water.

They sent us for more beer and when we came back one of the miners was telling them all about his brother who worked on the farm that belonged to some professor from the University in Edinburgh. The word was that he was doing experiments to cross horses and donkeys with zebras and the like – it was something to do with pack animals for Africa – and they were all coming up with daft names for what you might call such a thing: zonkey was one I remember that made me giggle, hebra, zorse, dobra.

The train stopped at Peebles as usual on the way up to Penicuik and the station was busy; the platform was full. It turned out that a family were emigrating to Australia and they were getting on our train. It was a mother and father and two small girls, the older one would be about four. Their family and friends were all there to say cheerio and I could see them shaking hands, getting kisses and cuddles, the little ones not quite sure what was going on, and then what must have been the couple's mothers and fathers hanging on to them for grim death for a good minute or two when it came to their turn. I didn't really understand it then, I just thought it must be exciting for them to be starting a new adventure in a new country but their families would know that, like as not, they'd never see them again. They got themselves settled in the carriage next to ours. I could see hands waving out the window. I heard people shout cheerio and good luck, safe journey and God speed, and then I could see that the man in the train had a tight hold of someone's hand. This person had to run to keep up and I was worried in case the train was going to pull his arm off when, just as they got to the end of the platform, the man inside let go and his friend was left looking down the length of the train as it pulled away.

Just before you get to Penicuik you pass Wellington, the Reform School – the bad boys' school we always called it. No matter whether we were boys or not that's what we were threatened with if we misbehaved. Sometimes you'd see some of the boys out doing gym or sawing up wood. I always wondered what bad things they'd done to end up there. Sometimes you saw them in Penicuik with their blue corduroy shorts and I'd get a row for staring.

When we got off the train, Jess's sister, Chrissie, was there to meet us; Jess was waiting at the house. I remember how cold Chrissie's cheek felt when she kissed us. We followed her out of the station and along the road when we came face to face with a man and a greyhound – it would be a lurcher, but it looked like a greyhound. Well, did that not start Helen off? It wasn't two weeks since two big dogs had killed her kitten. We thought of it as Helen's kitten although it didn't live with us. It was one of Phamie's cat's kittens that they'd kept and Phamie's mother, seeing how keen Helen was to have one, had said that she could think of it as hers and come and see it any time she liked. She even let her pick its name; Twister she called it. Every day she'd be round to give it its dinner, feed it saucers of milk. She'd hide tasty bites off her plate and take them round. It would jump all over her, dig its claws into her chest and nuzzle her face. And then one day, we'd just come in from the school when we heard the most terrible commotion outside. We came out of the door and could see Big Alex running about after two greyhounds, roaring and shouting at them to let go. A young boy had a hold of them both but he was being pulled all over the place and looked terrified. When he caught sight of me and Helen, Big Alex shouted at us to get back in the house, but just then, just the way the dogs turned, we could see what it was that they had. Nothing I could do; Helen took off, and the next thing she was battering hell out of these two dogs – battering their behinds and screaming at them to let go. Phamie's mother was out by this time and got a hold of her and dragged her into the house. Big Alex was angry, the boy was far too young to be let out with two big dogs like that and them not even muzzled. He went round to the boy's father and give him a piece of his mind but just got a load of cheek. So he reported it to the police and I think they must have had a word because the boy's father only ever walked them himself after that and they both had muzzles on. Too late though as far as the kitten was concerned. It had been sitting on the spar of the gate, right at the same height as the dogs' heads. Instinct I suppose; the nearest dog would just grab it.

Inconsolable doesn't even begin to describe Helen in the days after. She'd burst into tears at the least little thing. My granny skelped her for it but that just made her cry more. She'd scream that she wished she lived with Jess or Phamie, that she'd as soon live in the Poor House. My grandfather did his best to keep the peace although his breathing was worse by then. That's enough, away into your bedroom was about as much as he could muster.

The street in Penicuik wasn't like the last time we were up. It was just like any Friday: women doing their shopping, stuff being delivered, people going about their business as usual. That all changed when we got to Jess's. A good few neighbours were already in the house and Jess's friend Sadie with her mother, Jess's mother and father, my aunties and uncles who lived round about, so many that we couldn't see Jess when we went in at first. But then she appeared out of the front room. Her face crumpled when she saw us and she gave us both a big cuddle. Do you not think they are too young for a day like this, Jenny, she said to my granny, but my granny just shook her head and said it wouldn't do us any harm in the long run to see what life was about. He was our father and we were all he had. Other people came out of the front room that had been in to pay their respects. The door was open and we could see the side of the coffin. Is that our Dad? Helen asked and we both edged away from the door at the thought. Yes, she said, that's him but you don't need to go in there.

He's all covered up, the lid's shut, no-one can see him. And I remember there was a strong smell of carbolic and a fusty smell underneath it that just wasn't the smell of Jess's house at all because it always smelt fresh.

Next thing, we were in the kitchen and my Aunty Nellie had us organised with a drink of tea and a sandwich to keep us going because it was a cold day and we'd had no dinner. Then the Minister came and there was a service in the house. The Minister didn't come across as the friendliest of people but he did his job. During any prayers that were said I kept my eyes open and, during one of them, the hearse arrived; I saw it go by the window and stop so that I could still see the back of it. It was the feathers on the horses' heads that had caught my eye. I noticed that Jess was staring at the window too. She took a sharp breath in and her hand went up to her mouth as if to hold it all in. When the Minister had finished saying what a terrible thing it was, that Jesus had gone to prepare a place for us, and how we could all look forward to the resurrection, someone let the undertakers in. Jess kissed her fingers and touched the coffin as it went past and out the door.

The undertakers didn't seem to have much of a job lifting it onto the back of the hearse. In my head it was a skeleton they loaded onto their wagon. The horses were both black, both shining in what sunlight there was, their manes and tails brushed and braided, big ostrich plumes on their heads. And the hearse gleamed it was so polished, and the glass too. By the time we all got out and organised behind it they had the flowers in beside the coffin and some more people had arrived to walk with us to the cemetery. My granny had us well warned not to make a show of ourselves. We walked one on either side of her. Jess was in front with her mother and father and her sister. I was proud of how smartly she walked behind the hearse even though her eyes were on the coffin and the look on her face was heartbreaking. The only time I saw her turn her head was when we went in through the cemetery gates. There was a crowd of people there and I'll never forget the way she looked at one of them. When the horses stopped and the undertakers opened the hearse to unload the coffin, she walked across and spoke to a sober looking, well-dressed man. You could see his face go grey. Turns out he was the manager of the mine. She told him that he wasn't welcome at my Dad's graveside and that she'd appreciate it if he'd stay away. I didn't know that at the time. I was just struck by the dignified way she did it. Then we followed the coffin from the gate to the graveside.

A terrible feeling came over me. All I wanted to do was run away. One look from my granny was enough to put that thought out of my head. I put my hand up for her to take a hold of it but she didn't and I'd no option but to fall in with her and Helen as we walked up the path to the top of the cemetery where we could see at least three fresh-dug graves. It's funny how you remember things. What stuck in my head was the sound of people being quiet: their feet on the path, clothes rustling as they walked, muffled coughs and murmurs, whispering. For the rest of my life that kind of subdued noise has had the same effect as scraping a metal spoon on the inside of a pan. I still have nightmares where all of a sudden I'll be in the middle of such a crowd.

So that was the finish. That was him buried, my poor Dad. At the time all I felt was sheer bloody terror. I didn't know that's what it was. All I knew was that I couldn't stop my knees knocking and I felt queasy, a bit light-headed and that I didn't half jump at the sound of the first lot of earth that they flung into the grave. Helen started to shake her head and say, not my Dad, not my Dad. But my granny shook her by the arm and told her to wheesht. So I tried to catch her eye, tried to let her know that she still had me. Even although she was older, it often seemed like it was me looking after her. I always said it was because she was too nice but really it was because she was too sensitive, it was as if she had a layer missing and that wasn't a good thing when you lived with my granny. After my Dad was buried it was as if I didn't care what people thought and that included my granny. It was as if I'd grown an extra layer – I got to be just that little bit more stubborn, just that little bit more defiant; more devilment crept in. I stopped worrying about the poor house. If they took us away or my granny threw us out, I would go to stay with Jess. I took a leaf out of True Thomas' book. I spoke my mind.

Miss Lillie had read us the story of Thomas the Rhymer. I'd pestered her ever since Big Alex had spoken about it – anything to do with Phamie's brother, Tom, and I was interested. I was fascinated by the Queen of the Faeries. I loved to hear what she looked like when Thomas first saw her, her horse decked out with bells hanging from its mane and jingling as she comes down the path; it still sends a shiver through me. I was so taken with the story I would go on and on about it at night in my bed. I wanted the fairies to be real. I wanted to go to the Eildons to see if I could get inside to see them. My plan was to get the train to Melrose and camp out on the hillside. I'd eat the supper that I'd take with me – it was to be a boiled egg and a lemon curd sandwich – and wait for it to get dark because that was when the fairies came out. The Faerie Queen would be beautiful, kind and gentle and lift me up on her horse. All the bells would tinkle as we rode into an opening in the hillside and I'd have the most fantastic night, I'd dance to the liveliest music, eat and drink the tastiest and most delicious things you could ever imagine. Many's a night that thought saw me off to sleep. Helen would always be worrying about how the fairies lived under the ground: what kind of lights did they have; how did the earth not just fall down on top of them; where did their water come from; what did they feed the horses on? Then she would get upset about the horses down the mine. She couldn't stand the thought of them living under the ground. My Dad hadn't helped, telling her about the time when they first got the horses in Mauricewood, not that long before the Disaster. Three horses they took down, put them in a harness, lifted them right up in the air and loaded them into a crate that they lowered down the mineshaft. Two of them had been quiet but one had put up a struggle and made such a racket that someone had shouted, shoot the bugger. But they'd got it down and it had settled when it saw the other ones. Helen had been up to ninety at the thought of these horses never seeing the sun or a patch of green ever again. My Dad had to tell her that they'd only be there for a while and they'd bring them back up, retire them to a farm that had big fields full of the juiciest grass, and get a new lot. Poor things were killed in the Disaster along with the men. The rescuers had to clamber over them to get to some of the bodies. It was two of the pony drivers who went to warn the miners about the fire, them and another boy. They'd been bringing the ponies back for their morning feed when one of them discovered the fire. He was one of the last they found, and in a terrible mess at the bottom of the sump.

Anyway, my truth-telling got me into a hell of a bother. I told my granny: I don't think God'll be too pleased to see the way you're carrying on; me and Helen would like some meat if you're having some; we were dancing round at Phamie's; Jesus wouldn't want to have anything to do with you, you're a Gentile (I must've heard the word at the Sunday School). And outside I'd be saying things like: no, I couldn't do that or I'd get a hiding; my granny says that Alex'll burn in hell for not believing; Helen got that black eye when my granny pushed her out of bad temper. My granny was spitting mad but that was one of the good things about living in a small town, for good or ill, people knew each other's business; it made her think twice when she lost her temper. My grandfather was relieved as much as affronted. It made things better for him too. And it gave my granny a good excuse to act the martyr; her own turning against her after all she'd done for them. Just like the funeral had given her a great excuse to parade her tragedy in front of a crowd. And there was a fair crowd at the graveside.

I don't remember very much about what happened after the burial; it gets mixed up with the first time we went up. There was definitely a tea in the Free Church Hall put on by Jess's mother and her friends. But first we looked at the flowers. We had a minute or two to think before people came to speak to Jess and to my granny. They smiled at me and Helen with pathetic looks on their faces. Me being me, I got sick of this and wouldn't look at anyone. I turned away from them and looked across to the hills trying not to listen to the terrible sounds that mourners make. I stuck my fingers in my ears when it was too much for me to bear and got a dunt from my granny. That's when I noticed that there was something stuck in Helen's hair. I pulled it out and realised that it was a broken piece of ostrich feather. It was so soft and delicate that instead of throwing it away, I held onto it and wrapped it up in my handkerchief. Then, when I got home, I put it into my special things box.

Coming down through the Crow Wood at the foot of
Caerlee was a procession the likes of which Martha
had never seen. She'd heard it first; it had woken
her up. She thought she'd heard the wind rustling
through dry beech leaves. But it wasn't that at all;
it was something wondrous. It was the sound of a
thousand fairy horse hooves and the tinkling of the
ten times as many silver bells that hung from their
bridles. At the head of the procession, on a dapple
grey, was the fairest woman that Martha had ever set
eyes on. Her flaxen hair, crowned with a circlet of rose
and jessamine, hung down past her waist. She had on
a dress of the greenest green but so light and airy that
Martha could see the sheen of her milk white skin
beneath it. About her shoulders, and falling in drifts
across her horse's back, was a velvet mantle as dark as
the needles of the Scots pine that blotted the hillside,
clasped together at her throat by gold filigree set with
amber. On her feet were shoes of kid leather so soft
that Martha's first thought was to pull them from
her and go dancing between the trees. Will-o'-the-
wisp darted about in front of the horses lighting the
way because the darkness was creeping in. Martha
couldn't think how it had got to be so late. She'd been
picking rasps in the warm sunshine and had only sat
down for a minute to eat some. But as the riders came
nearer Martha felt no fear. Even in the gloaming she
could hear the songs of the missel thrush and the
blackbird, the jay and the wood pigeon, and their
music lifted her heart so that she jumped up, clapped
her hands and shouted you must be the Queen of the
Fairies because I've never seen lovelier.

As one, the procession stopped and a great silence
fell about the woods. The silver and gold and precious
jewels that were arrayed about the company cast a

weird gleam out of which Martha heard a silken voice
tell her that she was wrong. I am Peerie, the Queen of
the Dead, said the Queen of the Fairies. You look awful
cheery to be the Queen of the Dead, said Martha. The
Queen of the Fairies smiled. Aren't you told not to fear
death? I suppose so. Then see and believe, she said
gesturing to the host behind her, see and believe. In
that case, said Martha, have you seen my Dad? There
are many dead, said Peerie, too many for me to know.
But if you come with me I can help you find him.
Should I not be scared? If I go with you, will I have
to die? Not if you're with me. I'll keep you safe and
make sure you return to this place. Come, she said
and pulled Martha up behind her onto her horse. The
scents of rose and jessamine mingled with horse sweat
and the spicy dampness of the night wood. Martha's
hands closed tight round a waist that seemed smaller
than a waist should be; green velvet bulked under
her hands and warmth suffused through the delicate
material of the dress beneath it. Hold tight, shouted
Peerie as she urged on her horse, and the sounds of
tinkling bells merged with the drumming of horses'
hooves and the rush of the wind.

On and on they rode till they left behind all that was
familiar and came to a featureless plain. There they
came to a halt. Peerie jumped off her horse and pulled
Martha after her. I want to show you something, she
said. But first she held Martha in a tight embrace and
kissed her thrice upon the cheek saying that this was
her charm, her promise. Her lips felt cool and dry and
yet each kiss burst in a flurry of sparks on Martha's
skin. Holding Martha by the shoulders, she turned her
around and said do you see those three paths in front
of us? As Martha peered into the distance she could

see that the road split into three as it disappeared over the horizon. The first is the path of righteousness, said Peerie, and immediately she and Martha were on it. They could scarce stand side by side the path was so narrow. Gorse and briar prickled thick at either side where rosehips hung as random drops of red. The footway was rutted and muddy, jagged rocks stuck up through it and a fallen tree blocked the way. It takes a strong and determined person to navigate this path; not many people on earth come by here.

Now let us see the second path, and they stood on a broad, easy, handsome way. The sun shone, water lilies floated on a clear lake, the air was filled with the lazy hum of bees. Martha sighed as if relieved. This is the path of wickedness, said Peerie. She clasped Martha's shoulders tighter. But it looks like paradise, said Martha. Yes. Many think that this is the road to heaven but they are mistaken.

Come, let us make our way along the bonny road that winds up the bracken-covered hillside because that is the path that will lead us to our destination. And will my Dad be there, asked Martha? How long has he been dead? Scarce six months. Then he should be. But I have to warn you that tomorrow night is when the Devil comes to take his tithe and he favours the young and strong and the not long dead. We must ride fast to get there before the sun sets on the morrow.

On and further on they rode until they entered a land where there was neither sun nor moon, just a twilight that was at times as soft and delicate as the feathers on the breast of a collared dove, but that was at other times iron grey and full of foreboding. There they rode through rivers of blood up to the knee. When Martha asked where all this had come from, Peerie told her that all the blood that was ever shed ran through these rivers and emptied into the sea far, far away at a place where the very pebbles on the shore catch fire.

In time they came to a meadow bounded by trees near the top of a hill. The summer's grass was bleached out, spotted with the snow-like blooms of yarrow and the sudden yellows of coltsfoot. The trees bent into the wind against a sky streaked white above lowering clouds that faded to metalled lilac in the east. Peerie picked a rosy crab apple from its branch. Take this as my gift to you; it will give you a tongue that can never lie. But will that not just get me into bother? And anyway, are these not too bitter to eat? You need a heck of a sugar to make them taste good. Exactly, the memory of the taste will remind you of why the truth should always be told. From beneath another branch, Peerie produced a long coat of fine green tweed and a pair of green velvet shoes. It can be cold where we are going, she said. Put these on. Martha did as she was told and they rode off under a yellow-tinged sky whose grey ragged clouds darkened the outline of distant hills. They entered a wood. Branches around them swayed in a wind that tore at the outer edges of it. Fine rain turned heavy and silenced the chatter of small birds. Birches trembled between gusts; their small but frantic violence shook water droplets onto Martha's head and hands; their leaves scattered on the ground to fall as golden emblems on the sumptuous moss, while around and beyond them, spent bracken crumbled to rust amid falling structures of hogweed and burr. Martha thought that she saw the moon reflected in a pool of water but it was the creamy remains of a large fungus onto which water dropped with a sound like someone flicking paper.

They rode out of the woods at first light, the night's rain glass-seeding the windblown grass of the valley that lay before them. A low sun set a nearby copse of beech aflame and glittered in its wet branches. Peerie pointed towards a snaking geometry of stone walls that cut through the green of the valley. Do you see beyond the dykes where that smoke rises white? Yes, said Martha, although her gaze was distracted by three crows who alighted, squawking, onto a solitary, misshapen oak, the sun flashing silver on their backs. Our journey's end, said Peerie, and urged on her horse.

As they came near, Martha became aware of tendrils of white smoke in the air, which thickened to an opaque mist that smelled of cold. She shivered then gasped in fear when, out of the mist, rose a sheer wall of rock. Peerie's horse did not slow. Martha closed her eyes and waited for the impact, but none came. She opened them to see that they were in a rocky tunnel. The sound of the horses echoed and reverberated so that the sound was everywhere and everything, and Martha felt a strange sense of excitement bubble up inside her. Then they were out in the open, in a bright morning whose light Martha breathed in as if released from a prison. Peerie pulled up her horse and walked it to the edge of a rise. And there below them was an enormous castle, its high, high walls made of crystal. One hundred towers there were, whose arched buttresses rose sparkling out of a deep ditch. Huge metal doors decorated with images of diverse animals and studded with precious stones punctuated its facade. The roof was of burnished gold. It lit up the land around it as bright as the noonday sun.

The procession wound its way down from the ridge and across the valley towards it. At Peerie's arrival, the doors swung open but she turned aside, allowing those following her to enter first. And it was a strange procession that she welcomed. First came fierce-faced men armed with great swords and carrying many flags. Then came men and women quaintly dressed who passed quietly by, then musicians with tabours and trumpets and all kinds of minstrelsy, then a string of horses with no visible riders. These are they who have eaten of the fern seed, said Peerie when she saw Martha's puzzled face. Then sixty women in good spirits, each with a hawk on her hand that was sent to find game by the rivers, and much game had they found: mallard and heron and cormorant. Great poachers those, thought Martha as she and Peerie followed their laughter through the bejewelled doors and into a courtyard paved with white marble. And what a crowd there was within those sparkling walls of those who had been brought there dead and yet were not. Some stood without hands and some had no arms and some had grievous wounds. Their clothes had a white tinge and were stuck about with blots of paper. These had been paper mill workers. Some had guns and sat on horses, some lay strangled on the ground, their uniforms bore the arms of Napoleon. Then Martha saw a crowd of men and boys huddled together, some drowned in water and some with the scorch marks of fire on them. As she drew nearer she could see others among them that had bloody gashes and dark patches on their clothes where the blood had seeped. Some had bonnets and jackets, some had waistcoats and shirts. Some were quiet and some conversed with their neighbours. But some were laughing and that's when Martha saw him. Dad, Dad, she shouted and ran to hold him so tight it took her breath away. Dad, there's not a mark on you. How can you be dead? I just fell asleep and woke up here with the rest of them. And what a great time we've been having. They've been feeding us like kings and every night there's a party. And at that, trumpets sounded. There was a raucous clang of sharpening steel and in a doorway behind a table laden with dates and figs, damsons and hazelnuts, stood cooks with large fine-bladed knives such as butchers might use to dress a carcass. Forty roe deer were chased in by thin, long-legged hounds who were soon lapping at blood that flowed a startling red against the white of the floor. Harps and fiddles, whistles and ivory combs wrapped in fine tissue paper, pipes of oat, of hemlock large and small, and of bog reed played many a lively tune. The papermakers danced with the women of good spirits whose hawks flew above them on the ends of long jesses. Napoleon's soldiers danced with the cooks, the blood of the one's uniforms mingling with that of the other's aprons. The miners danced with the quiet women in their quaint dresses or with the children of the musicians. Martha danced with her Dad, the smell of him and the solid warmth of his hands in hers made her light-headed. Then Martha noticed that men in top hats appeared among the dancers. They seemed to dance alone as they partnered those who had eaten of the fern seed. Their dancing was clumsy. Martha wondered if they were drunk. They laughed too loud. They moved around the floor as if they had it to themselves. They bumped into the other dancers but never apologised. When they bumped into the miners, blood spurted from wounds that opened afresh or seeped from bodies that had known no injury. This horrified the quiet women and the children of the musicians. The word murderers echoed round the courtyard. Then the screaming started.

Martha was held fast by unknown hands as dancers and musicians ran from sight. It was Peerie whose hands held her tight. Stay with me, she said, fear nothing and no-one, as Martha turned towards the sound of a great commotion near the door. It was the Devil come for his tithe. Ten feet tall at least he stood, his body magnificent in its muscularity. His hair and beard were a writhing mess of fire. The light from them sparkled black-edged fiery rainbows off the crystal walls of the castle courtyard. Flames flickered over his chest, over his arms and legs which were the hind legs of a massive bull whose cloven hooves were so hard they sounded like gunshot as he walked. His eyes were jagged nuggets of jet that gleamed and repelled all looking. In his left hand was a three-pronged fork that Martha supposed was for poking sinners into the fiery pit. Each swish of his barbed tail sent up a shower of red sparks. No wonder people are scared, thought Martha, as the Devil let out a sound that was like the booming of a great engine.

On the far wall, a door opened. In came the fierce-faced knights. Then those who were quaintly dressed, the musicians and the sixty women with hawks. They all traversed the cold white space of the castle courtyard and filed into a door behind the dais on which stood Peerie, looking defiant, with Martha at her side. The Devil snorted and growled as he watched them pass. Then all grew quiet as the bloodied soldiers of Napoleon entered the room behind the mutilated paper mill workers. The Devil took a step forward, the sound of it ricocheting through the crystalline air. And as the men and boys of Mauricewood appeared before him, hot saliva ran from his mouth, turning to steam and falling as snow on the white marble.

Into that moment filtered the sweet, sweet sound of a child singing. It was Martha. Why weep ye by the tide, ladye, she sang, why weep ye by the tide, and for a moment, the Devil was entranced. A moment long enough for all the men and boys of Mauricewood to file behind the dais so that when the singing stopped and the Devil resumed his deadly choice, it was the men in the top hats who were passing.

You must leave now, said Peerie. But what about my Dad? I've only just found him. You must leave now or risk the wrath of the Devil. But I can't leave my Dad. You must go back now. Take this. Into Martha's hand, Peerie pressed a pretty stone in which the colour green circled itself in varying hues. This and the kiss I gave you earlier will protect you. Martha's tears splashed onto the green stone and turned to ice that shattered as it hit the floor. You weep now but take heed of what I say. There is a day coming when churches are used as stables and castles as hay barns, when all will be held to account and no heavenly being invoked to excuse. And then there will come a day when the sun no longer shines. Be kind. Love all things that will pass. Love all things that will pass... and keep a truthful head.

Martha woke in the woods at the foot of Caerlee, her face wet with tears, the songs of the missel thrush and the blackbird, the jay and the wood pigeon sounding the memory of her dream.

Jess: 5th September 1889

Jess: 5th September 1889

It was a nice September morning, a wee bit misty but the sun was there. We were both on early shifts so I gave him a kiss as usual when we got to the corner. I was going one way to the mill and he was going the other up the Edinburgh road. I always stood a minute and watched him. Sometimes he'd look back and wave but most times he'd be too busy blethering with them as he'd met and were on their way to the pit same as him. Many's the time since the Disaster I've pictured them that morning walking along the road laughing and joking, their piece boxes and flasks making bulges in their jackets, their hands in their trouser pockets against the early morning chill, kicking up dust as they walked past the fields and the big trees by Beeslack, the dust landing on the hedgerows that lined the hill up to Mauricewood.

Author's notes and acknowledgements

The Mauricewood Devils is based on events relating to the Mauricewood Pit Disaster of 5th September 1889. Mauricewood lies on the edge of the Lothian coalfield on the outskirts of Penicuik, Midlothian. A stone memorial on the Mauricewood Road records the names of the sixty three men and boys who died there – nineteen of them under twenty-one, the youngest twelve years old.

This retelling imagines the stories the wife and daughter of one of the victims might have told if they had ever been asked about it or if they had ever been inclined to tell. It was written out of curiosity as my great-grandmother's father was one of those killed but, as was the way with her generation, she never said much about the tragedies of her childhood; the only details I had were that they found his piece box floating in the water of the flooded mine and that she had twiddled the button of one of the soldiers who lined the streets of Penicuik for the largest of the funeral processions. She also told me how pleased she had been when her father bought her a pair of buttoning boots. She died when I was thirteen.

The Mauricewood Devils references oral narrative tradition in its presentation as monologue, in its allusion to ancient ballad, in the child Martha's fantasies, and in the presentation of factual material in fifty word paragraphs which exploit the contention that fifty is the maximum number of words that we as humans can memorise *verbatim* without recourse to the written word.[*]

[*] I. M. L. Hunter in Rubin, D. C. *Memory in Oral Traditions*, Oxford University Press, Oxford, 1997, p.6.

There are three or four fifty-word paragraphs per page reflecting the number of feet per line in traditional ballad metre. Numbers at the foot of each 50-word paragraph page refer to acknowledged sources as outlined below.

[1] *Mauricewood Disaster:* Mining in Midlothian by Andrew B. Donaldson

[2] *Mauricewood Burning!: The Centenary Story of Lothian's Worst Pit Disaster* by Fred Pringle

[3] *The Black Collection* at Local Studies and Archives, Midlothian Library Headquarters, Loanhead.

[4] National Mining Museum Scotland www.nationalminingmuseum.com

[5] *Inquiry under the Coal Mines Regulation Act, 1887, into the fatal accident which occurred at Mauricewood colliery on the 5th September 1889.*

Supplementary Report to the Secretary of State for the Home Department by Henry Johnston, Advocate, and Thomas Bell, one of Her Majesty's Inspectors of Mines

[6] Contemporary newspaper reports from the following: *Midlothian Journal, Dalkeith Advertiser, Glasgow Herald, Scotsman*

[7] *The Life and Work of Samuel Rutherford Crockett* by Islay Murray Donaldson

[8] The Franks Report to the Children's Employment Commission, 1842

[9] *The Gladstone Diaries Volume XII: 1887-1891, With Cabinet Minutes and Prime-Ministerial Correspondence* edited by Matthew (1994) 250w from pp.229-231 (By permission of Oxford University Press)

[10] *Oxford Dictionary of National Biography*

[11] *Uncontrolled Recirculation – the 1889 Mauricewood Disaster,* Colliery Guardian, May 1984, pp173-174, A. Gracie and B. Job

[12] The following works by Samuel Rutherford Crockett: *The Stickit Minister, The Lilac Sunbonnet, Vida, The Raiders, and Cleg Kelly (in particular for the inspiration for Big Alex)*

[13] *King James Bible*

[14] *Crime and Punishment,* F M Dostoyevsky

[15] Paragraphs constructed from combined sources

I am also indebted to the following for inspiration and factual detail:

www.scottishmining.co.uk; Penicuik Library; Joy Deacon, *The Mauricewood Pit Disaster;* National Museum of Scotland for information on miner's housing conditions; *Through the Mill, Personal Recollections by Veteran Men and Women Penicuik Paper Mill Workers* by Ian MacDougall; *The Annals of Penicuik* by John J Wilson; *Leithenside School Logbook,* Document P/Ed/2/15 in the archives of Scottish Borders Council, Heritage Hub, Hawick; *Glimpses of Old Innerleithen* and *Traquair* from the collection of R. B. Robb and E. R. Stevenson; *The Minstrelsy of the Scottish Border* by Sir Walter Scott.

[All efforts have been made to contact holders of rights and permissions.]

And appreciative thanks to Helen MacPherson, Martha's daughter; Doreen Robb, Martha's granddaughter; Margaret Coull, Penicuik Local History Society; library and archives staff; the Institute for Advanced Studies in the Humanities at the University of Edinburgh; the Scottish Arts Council for a Small Research Grant; all who read early drafts; all at Freight; and LJA as always.

www.dorothyalexander.co.uk